The Legend of the Zombie Pigman

Pigman

Book 1: The Beginning

(An Unofficial Minecraft Book)

By Cube Hunter

Copyright © 2021 by Cube Hunter

WWW.CUBEHUNTER.NET

Visit Us: CubeHunter.net

E-mail: support@cubehunter.net

Table of Contents

About the Author

CUBE HUNTER is a 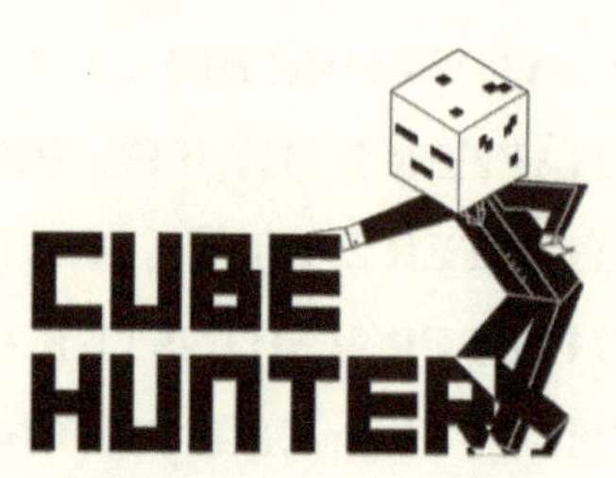 group of avid Minecraft players, fan-fiction readers, and incredible writers that aim to bring only the best stories to block-smashers of all ages. In a world filled with danger, weapons, tools, enemies, adventure around every turn, and, of course, blocks, Cube Hunter brings fans more depth to the wide-ranging characters that inhabit the Minecraft worlds.

And guess what? There's more in store. The team at Cube Hunter adores everything about Minecraft and is currently creating new adventures to be had by those who want to expand their block-filled horizons. Grab any copy of our incredible adventure tales, sit back, and enjoy exploring new worlds with new friends…and possibly some enemies too.

DO YOU LOVE FREEBIES?

Grab a free copy of our adventurous unofficial Minecraft fiction story!

Visit: WWW.CUBEHUNTER.NET

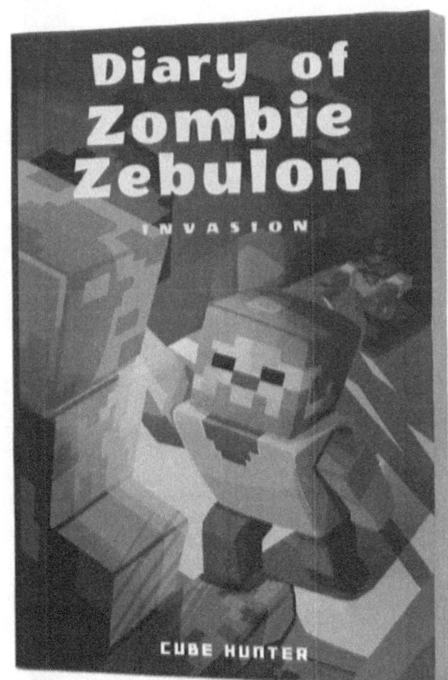

Chapter 1: Oh, the Pigs

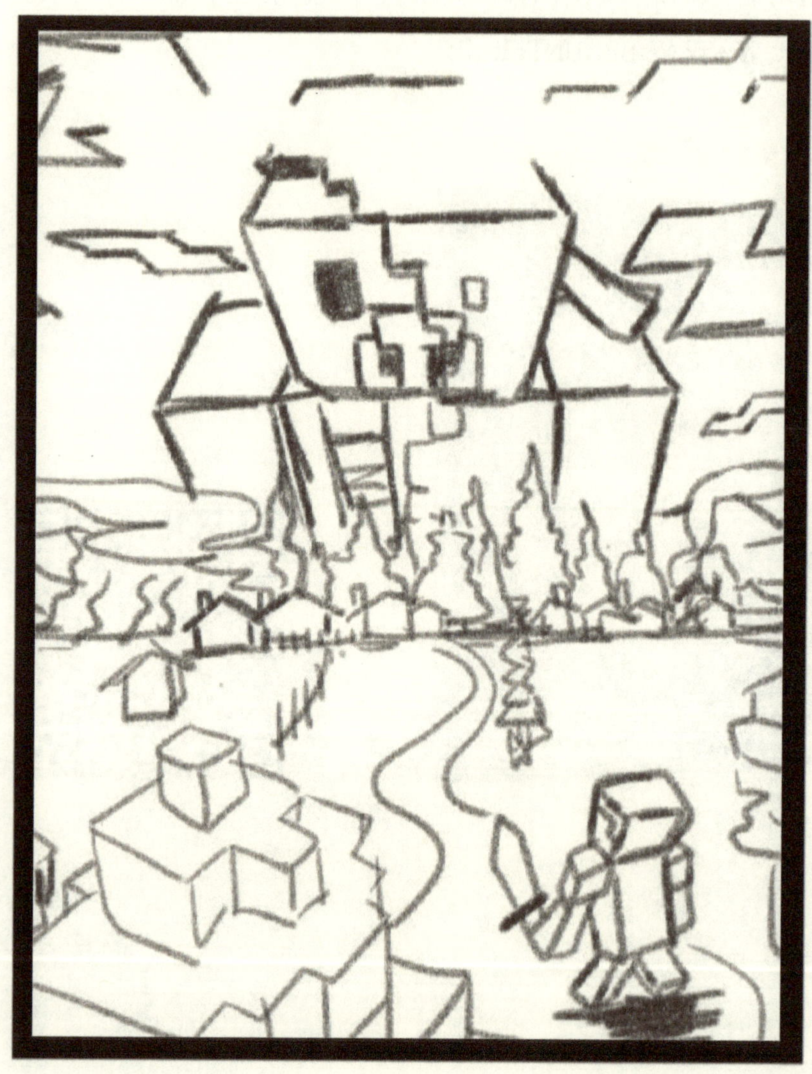

The life of a pig may sound boring, but it is everything except that. Strolling around the fields is quite hard work. You have to watch out for random craters that those creepers make. It is quite puzzling to them why creepers explode in the first place. You might not know this, but creepers are like cousins to pigs. That is why the pigs care so much about them.

Pigs are also quite smart. They always seem like they are going somewhere, but nobody knows where. They are very cautious of their surroundings as well. They will always avoid those one block drops because they have small feet. It is quite hard for them to climb that one block. You would know this if your feet were as small as theirs.

Pigs have a really hard time during the night. Who doesn't, after all? They, on the other hand, get spooked far too easily. The zombie lurking around the corner of that tree has the potential to startle that pig. The same thing happens when spiders fall from trees

Pigs are also very scared of the rain. The loud thunderstorms scare them a lot. There is also a legend among the pigs. A legend about their brethren, the Pigman! It's a scary story that all mama pigs tell their children.

There was once a pig who was the bravest of them all. He did not fear any jump scare zombies or any falling spiders. He was so brave that he would stroll around even during a thunderstorm. Every pig looked up to him and wanted to be like him. One day, it was raining very hard, and there were more thunderstorms than usual. But it didn't matter to our brave pig. He had his mind set on going somewhere.

It was a large plains biome. There were no trees anywhere, only a long stretch of semi flat-land and some occasional craters and ponds. Seeing that, our fellow pig felt a tug in his stomach. His instincts were telling him to wait out the storm. But despite this, he didn't lose his determination. "I have to do it!" he decided. After all, he could not show his weakness to the other pigs that were watching him; so he started his journey.

After he left his shelter from under the tree, he felt a sense of accomplishment for what he was doing. He was feeling proud of every step he was taking. But then came the disaster; a bolt of lightning struck him. He felt his health lower immediately. For a brief moment, everything went white, and his head felt light. He crawled to a nearby pool of water to see what had happened to him, and he couldn't believe what he saw with his own two eyes.

Two of his front limbs had turned into hands. His face was half pig and half skeleton; and worst of all, he had green marks all over his body, like a zombie. He was so devastated that he did not want to continue his journey anymore and turned back.

Meanwhile, the other pigs were watching him from under the trees. They were extremely concerned about what happened to their fellow pig. But soon, that concern turned into terror. They saw what he had become and were immediately scared of him. When he returned, he tried to convince them that he was the same despite his looks, but nobody would listen to him. They all just ran away from him without giving him a chance to talk.

After all of this, he was extremely sad and lonely. He had nobody to watch all his brave acts, no other fellow pigs to talk to. All he did was travel around. Until one day, he found a mysterious gate.

There was solid black obsidian that formed a strong rectangular frame with a purple glass that appeared to be moving within it. He mustered the courage to put one of his hands in it. His hand passed through. He couldn't hold it any longer. Curiosity got the best of him, and he went inside. After that, no one saw anything else.

Some pigs did find this story inspiring, while others find it terrifying. It sparks equal amounts of bravery and cowardice among the pigs. Some say that it is a story of the legends, and it isn't true, while others are strong believers of this story.

To this date, a few brave pigs follow the legacy of that pig. They travel through all of the overworld without any fear. Those who suffer the same fate as the first pigman are said to search for that same portal to join their brethren and continue their adventure in a hellish and ruthless landscape called the Nether.

Chapter 2: Miss Alex Pax

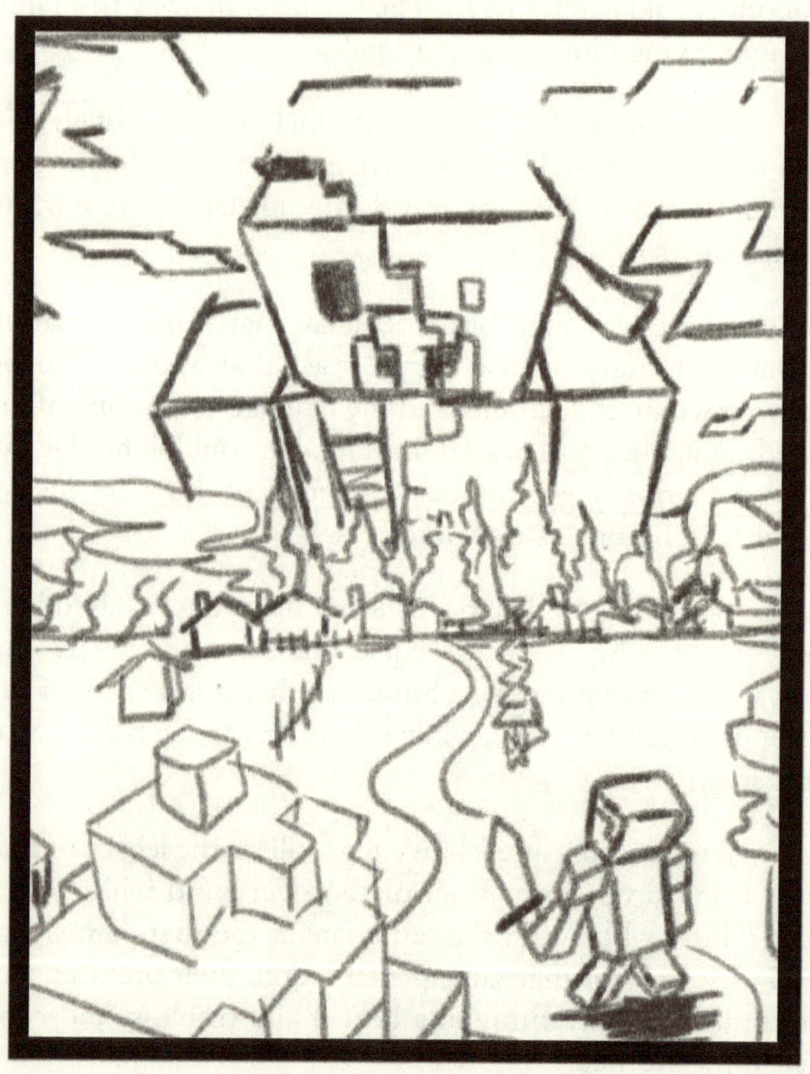

Alex was especially fond of pigs. She had a farm of pigs, but it wasn't what you would consider a farm. She did not put her pigs in those tight cages made of fences. What she did was the opposite. She let her pigs roam around wildly. She often feeds them, and she thinks they are attached to her. Well, who are we to tell her otherwise?

She also has a huge potato farm, but it is not for what you might think. See, pigs really love potatoes. And nobody knows it better than Alex. She especially loves it whenever she holds out a potato and the pigs rush over to her. She has lost count of how many pigs she has fed over the years. She never gets annoyed by them.

We could sit here all day asking her about the things she likes about pigs, and she still wouldn't finish. It's just that they are pink. Their eyes are big and dreamy. And they have small, cute feet. They move in a funny but cute way. She just adores them, and her heart just melts whenever they eat potatoes from her hand.

She also breeds a lot of pigs. She really loves the baby pigs. They are just too cute for her to handle. She always looks for opportunities to talk about pigs. Day in, day out, all she probably thinks about is pigs.

On the other hand, she really can't stand any cows. To her, cows just seem too obnoxious. They are too loud, and whenever she tries to feed them, they seem to try to bite her whole hand off. She doesn't like it when they make loud sounds. According to her, the only thing going for the cows is that they produce milk. And milk is essential for something she loves making. Cakes!

Alex loves cakes because they are very pretty and taste amazing. She makes a lot of them and has a storage room where there are double chests full of cakes. She eats them all the time. She says that even if she eats a billion cakes, she will not get tired of them.

Steve wasn't particularly fond of cakes. Alex and Steve would constantly argue about cakes. "Cakes are so impractical. They take up so much space. You could take bread or steaks instead. They take up way less space and are efficient." It wasn't the taste that bothered Steve. He just found it unreasonable to carry cakes around. "Cakes taste way better than bread or steaks. My cakes are the best. It takes more space because it is tastier than your steaks, Steve. That's how you know they are better." Alex's logic never made sense to Steve.

Alex also has a huge chicken farm where she gets her eggs. She has neutral feelings about chickens. They are not as loud and noisy as cows, but they are also not as cute as her pigs. Well, they are cute, but they just eat the seeds and then run away. They are pretty hard to catch. The little chicks, however, are a different case. Most of them don't run away from you. They are cute and small and will play with you if you give them seeds.

She also has a flourishing wheat and sugarcane farm. She is especially proud of that wheat farm. It was the first farm she ever made. Then, she didn't know how to till the soil and what to plant. And somehow, she kept ruining her crops. It took her about a full Minecraft month to learn how to grow the fields properly and harvest the crops.

Alex's life was nothing too extravagant. She had a small, cute cottage-esque house. She liked to feed her pigs and cows and chickens during the morning and tended to her farms during the day. After gathering all the ingredients all day, she would relax and make cakes in the evening.

Chapter 3: Monster Hunter Steve

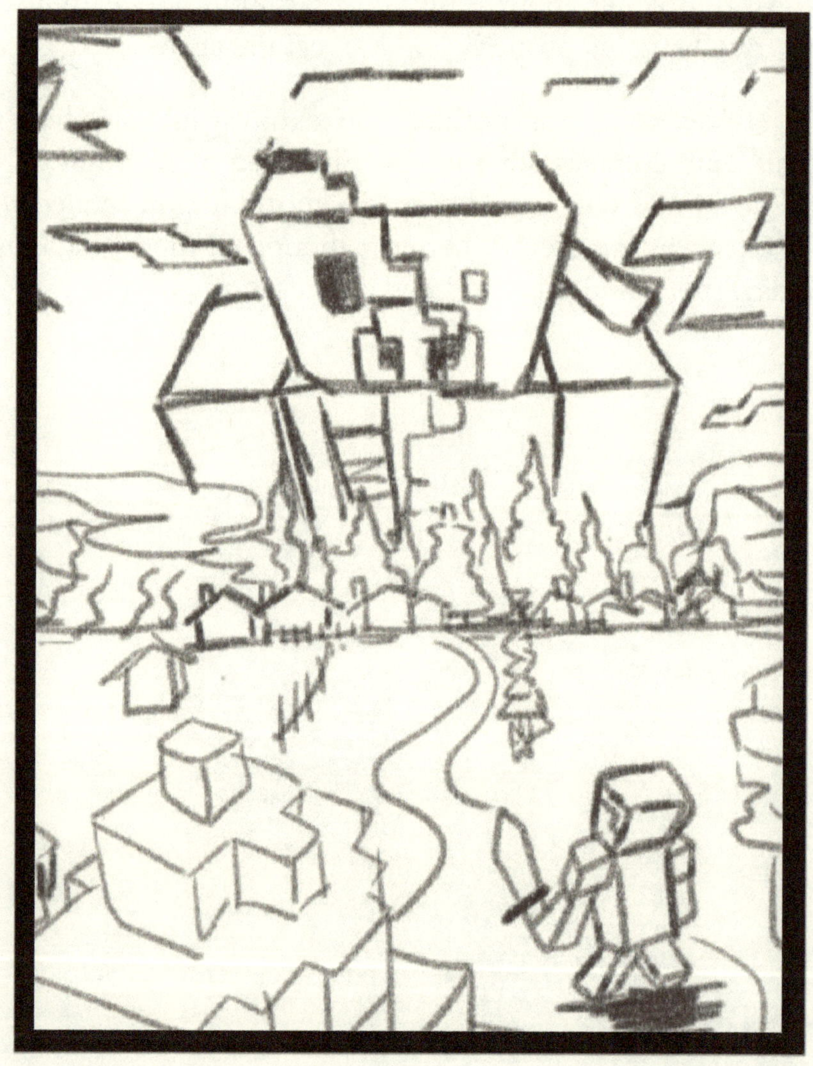

Alex loved her animals and her farms. She lived a modest life and loved to just relax at the end of the day. Steve, on the other hand, loved adventure and travelling. Instead of sleeping through the night, he loved the thrill of killing mobs, a torch in one hand, and a sword in the other. He was not the one to cower behind a shield.

Steve didn't become a zombie-killing maniac on his first night. He used to be more afraid than Alex, and he never strolled alone. But then, one day, he crafted an iron sword for himself. He did not totally steal it from Alex. He swung around and killed a few zombies. The zombies hit him back, but that did not stop him. After killing about eight zombies, he fled as his health was low.

"You are so careless all the time," Alex would say to him. "Don't take the monsters lightly. Things will turn bad if you do." It was Steve's first time and he underestimated them. "Yeah, my bad," Steve replied. "Take things more seriously!" Alex scolded him. "You need to get rid of that carefree attitude. You almost died because you were way too confident. Practice with the sword first then go fight the monsters. Don't act like an idiot." Steve finally understood how serious Alex was. She can be quite scary if she wanted to. As for Steve, his future exploits went way better, except for one time. We will talk about it later.

He did not have any armor or a shield protecting him, but only a trusty sword in his hand. He fell in love from the first swing. He loved the thrill and loved the risk. Some would call him a wild madman, but he was anything but that.

He was precise with a sword and so accurate with the bow that he never missed a shot.

The bow was his necessity as he didn't sleep at night. This was because of the phantoms hunting him down. No matter how much Alex scolded him, he just didn't like to sleep. He occasionally slept whenever Alex could persuade him. In those dark nights, when those phantoms attack, he knows that he has a bow he can trust. Well, almost every time.

Once, he forgot to make extra arrows for the phantoms. The zombies came in hordes, and so did the spiders. There were a few more skeletons than usual, but it was nothing he couldn't handle. Zombies came, and he slew them. His bow was as accurate as always, and his sword was swinging with nothing but perfection. But then came the phantoms, swooshing from the skies and hitting Steve. As he pulled his bow out to shoot, he saw he had no arrows left.

It was an impossible scenario. Zombies surrounded him, and skeletons sniped him as he fought with the phantoms. His hearts dropped quickly. He made a run for it. He dodged the skeletons, but the phantoms kept hitting him. Finally, with one last sprint, he made it into Alex's house. Half a heart. That was how low he was.

From then on, he was always careful to pack an extra half a stack of arrows that he reserved for only when phantoms attacked him. And he also came to another realization that he should probably build a house for himself.

Now, Steve wasn't as patient as Alex and felt that his house needed to be more practical than pretty.

So, what we call his house is a massive cube filled to the brim with chests and chests. He has an equally large basement with an array of furnaces set up for when he needs to mass melt something. He also has a very secret room under his basement, and only he knows how to get there. It is so hidden that even he sometimes forgets that it is even there.

Alex was quite a bit annoyed by this. She had a beautiful cottage in a perfectly picturesque place, and a few blocks away was this huge stone box. Well, she couldn't complain as Steve was her only companion. They might be completely different from each other, but they get along really well. They had this amazing synergy with a contrast of calm and chaos.

Chapter 4: The Journey to a Village

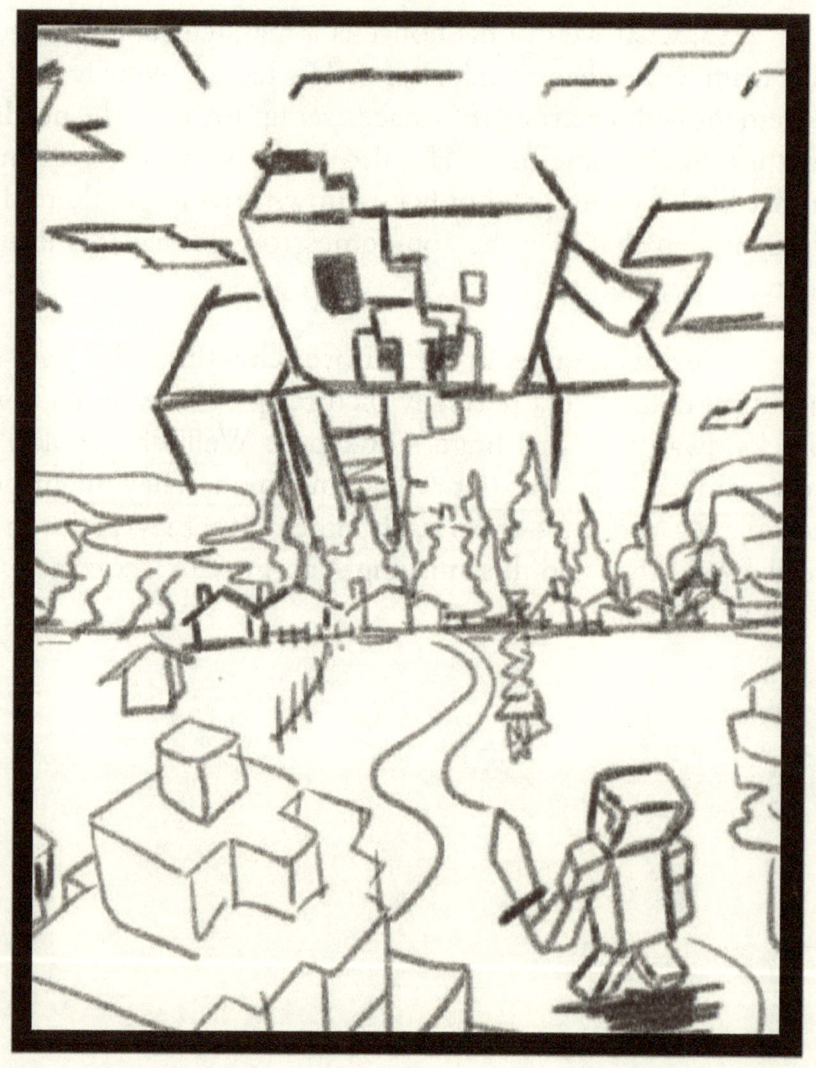

Alex was really grateful to have Steve by her side. He might have been that scaredy-cat once, but now he helps protect her farms and her pigs. Steve went on adventures and took care of the mining duties for her. And occasionally, he would even bring her gifts. He once even brought her a diamond.

These days, it isn't much different. Steve still roams around, killing monsters, and exploring caves, while Alex tends the farms and the animals. Until recently, Steve comes home all excited.

"I have found something really interesting. Something I had never seen before," he told her. "I could have found a village of some sort! It seems like there are a lot of wooden houses and I think I also saw some villagers. There might be some other people out there!" Steve was breathing heavily from excitement.

Alex became ecstatic after hearing this but was still a little skeptical. She told him, "I thought there weren't any more people out there except us. "Yeah, me too. But it might not be like that. I am sure there were other people there. We might not be alone in this overworld," Steve explained. "But isn't it too weird that people randomly appeared out of nowhere? There are just way too many things that don't add up." Alex was convinced that this wasn't going to end up well.

"Come on, Alex. You never go out on adventures anyways. Trust me this time. I am really sure it is a village.

You won't regret it." He was trying his best to convince her. She reluctantly agreed. "Don't tell me when things go wrong because I have already warned you." Alex was usually not this stubborn. It was that she was willing to go but wanted to make sure that everything was right. Don't get her wrong; she would rather avoid such adventures and live her peaceful life. But this time, it was a bit different. This time she might get to meet new people.

As it was already pretty late, they decided to start out the next day. Alex prepared extra cakes. Steve double-checked his armor and sword's durability so that they wouldn't fail him when he needs them. Alex also crafted a fresh new set of leather armor as they were more comfortable than iron. Soon night fell, and it was one of those rare nights where Steve actually slept. He did not want any phantoms chasing him.

When morning came, Steve prepared extra food and crafted an extra set of swords. He crafted a bow and a few arrows for Alex. Meanwhile, Alex was putting out chests outside. She completely filled one of them with arrows and put a sign in front of it that said: "Food here, piggies ." No matter how much Steve said that pigs couldn't open chests, she insisted on leaving food in them. He eventually gave up trying to convince her.

Soon it was time to head out. Alex's inventory was filled with cakes and potatoes. At least she had enough sense to bring a stack of blocks, her swords, and the bow and arrows Steve made. Steve's inventory was decked out with all the necessities. Full iron armor, two swords, his diamond pickaxe, and his favorite bow. He also had two stacks of blocks and two stacks of food he probably didn't need because Alex was bringing all the cakes and a boat.

"Are you sure you want to bring all those cakes?" Steve asked Alex. "Of course. The last thing you want is to be hungry," she replied. Steve didn't try to tell her anything that would make her upset. So, he just nodded and dropped the topic. "I wish Alex would stop being crazy over the cakes," he thought to himself. Well, it didn't matter much. It was time for them to start their adventures.

They were excited about starting their journey. But they knew it was going to be a long one. Alex took one look back at the pigs, and she was ready to go. "The village is out in the east. It would be at least 2000 blocks away," Steve estimated. They will have to fight through at least two nights. Well, all these thoughts didn't matter as they were already sprinting through the forest.

Soon, night fell. And then Alex remembered, "We didn't bring any extra torches, did we?" The only torch they had was the one Steve was holding in his other hand. It was dark fast, and they started hearing zombies around them. They had to prepare themselves to fight off the horde that was coming towards them. For Steve, it was just like another Saturday night. But for Alex, it was quite tough. With no light and little experience in wielding a sword, she struggled.

As comfortable as her leather armor was, it was not doing too well with blocking the hits. "Argh!" she grunted. She was having trouble fending off the zombies. That night, they were especially unlucky because soon, the baby zombies came. Baby zombies are much faster and ten times harder to kill. This was not helping Alex. Steve soon noticed this. "Watch out for the babies. They are really fast!" Steve was trying to help Alex as well as defending himself from the zombies.

When you are alone killing monsters, it is quite easy as the only thing you should keep in mind is not getting hit. But when protecting someone else, that task becomes way more difficult. Not only do you have to protect yourself, but you also have to protect another person. And you also had to make sure not to hit him as well.

Even Steve was having trouble doing all that. Alex was helping out somewhat, but that was not enough. Suddenly, Alex remembered her bow. She took it out. Instead of ramming headfirst with a sword, she fell back and started shooting arrows. "I will try to cover you with the bow," she suggested. "Watch out for the zombies behind you as well." Steve was quite concerned about her. It was not easy to hit moving targets with arrows. And the baby zombies didn't make it any better. They were fast, like really, really fast. It was extremely hard to hit them.

After skirmishing for what felt like an eternity, they finally caught a glimpse of the first rays of the morning sun. They knew they had to just hold on a bit longer. And soon, the sun rose, setting every monster on fire. They were happy, but they still had to be cautious as the monsters could now set them on fire as well. So, they kept dodging the monsters, and soon, all of the monsters were gone. They could finally take a breath of relief.

"Tough night, eh?" Steve said jokingly, but Alex wasn't amused. "Wow, that was tough. You all right, Alex?" Steve asked. "I am fine. Don't worry about me." She seemed quite grumpy. She was really disappointed in herself for being so useless.

Both of them sighed. The night was a lot rougher than it should've been. Alex started blaming herself. "Only if I could swing the sword properly, this wouldn't have happened." Steve reassured her, "It could've gone better. But I do enjoy a tough fight from time to time. It's fine, don't stress too much about it. I will figure something out so that this doesn't happen again." Alex still felt really bad for not being able to help out.

Steve just kept telling her that it was fine. "Trust me. It could have gotten a lot worse." But he knew if things kept going like this, his armor wouldn't hold up for more than a few nights. He had to figure out the problems and started finding solutions fast.

Firstly, Alex didn't have any torches. So, it was nearly impossible for her to see anything properly. He had to address this before anything else. "You need torches," he told Alex. "It would have made things a lot easier." Alex agreed with him. They had to get some before nightfall.

They had trees everywhere, but they needed coal. Steve remembered that there was a mountain biome nearby, and he could probably find some coal there. "Let's check out those mountains up ahead. We might get lucky and find some coals," he told her. And so, both of them made their way towards the mountain biome. Not much later, they could see the huge mountain peaks piercing the skies.

Finding the mountains wasn't the hard part but climbing them was. The mountains in that part were especially steep. Well, they had to do what they had to do. And it is to climb that mountain. So they started their slow ascent towards the peak. Thankfully, both of them had an adequate amount of blocks to make their climb a bit easier. But it was still quite a tough job.

Some of you might think, why didn't they just search for a cave? It would have been way easier to get into a cave, and there is usually an abundance of coal there. But remember, Alex couldn't fight very well. They also didn't have any extra torches. There were way too many uncertainties in a cave. And above all, Steve could not risk wasting any more of his armor's durability fighting monsters in a cave just to get some coal.

So, even though climbing a mountain is a tedious process, it's the better of the two choices. "This almost feels worse than fighting the monsters," Steve complained. It took them a painfully long time to reach the top. They couldn't rush it as one small mistake, and they would fall and have to start all over again. Slowly, they made progress. And eventually, they reached the peak. "Finally!" Alex exclaimed, clearly exhausted after all that. Both of them laid down to catch their breaths.

Thankfully, they didn't have to search for long before they found a huge strip of coal. Steve mined it with his pickaxe and made a lot of torches with the sticks Alex had. "Now, we will not run out of torches anytime soon." Steve was relieved. That solves one of their problems. Steve also made a shield for Alex. "Here, you will be able to block a lot more hits with the shield," he explained. Alex took the shield. It felt very clunky in her hands, but at least it would somewhat protect her. Steve tried to convince her to wear iron armor as it was stronger, but she didn't budge. It was just too heavy for her liking.

The view from the peak was breathtaking. It was unlike anything Alex had seen before. "Wow!" She was in awe of the beauty of nature. The sky was mesmerizingly golden with hues of purple, pink, and red. The other mountains and the waterfall looked amazing in the fading sunlight. The water sparkled like jewels, and there was a damp, pleasant smell in the air. Steve finally told Alex, "Hey, we don't have much time to awe over the beauty of that scenery as sunset means that it's gonna get dark soon." This really ruined her mood. Ste started to get worried.

As the sun was slowly setting, Steve got to thinking about how he could prevent the same thing from happening again. Suddenly, a small thought came to his mind. If Alex is more vulnerable to getting hit, she should stay somewhere safe instead. The gears in his mind slowly started turning. And finally, he thought of a strategy.

He quickly explained his idea to Alex, and they started to get to work. They didn't have much time. As they were way up on the mountain, the number of mobs spawning would be relatively less. So, he thought of making a tower for Alex where she can use her bow to shoot at the monsters. She could help him in killing them quickly while being safe herself.

They built it quickly with the stones Steve had. Alex made some fences around the platform so that she wouldn't accidentally fall down. Just as they finished, they started hearing zombies. Steve quickly placed a lot of torches and lit up the area. Alex was holding her bow, ready to rain down a barrage of arrows on anyone that comes near. "Come in my way to get shot, you zombies!" Alex screamed. Steve was surprised to see Alex being so enthusiastic. Everything already seemed way better than before. Steve drew his sword, and a horde of zombies rushed towards them.

This time it really was different. Not having to protect someone else, Steve was dueling flawlessly. Zombies approached and fell. A few skeletons also appeared, but Alex took quick care of them. She did miss some shots, but not being under pressure improved her aim significantly.

Everything was going smoothly. Steve's strategy worked. Soon there were no zombies or skeletons left. They fully lit up the peak so that no more could spawn. The night was finally going to be peaceful.

It was all quiet till sunrise. The view was equally breathtaking. But they couldn't waste much time. "Let's get out of here. We still have a long way to go," Steve told Alex. They had to get down from the mountain and clear out that desert biome. If they get stuck in the desert, it would be bad news. Luckily, they had a river stream near the base of the mountain. It was really good for them as they could travel in a boat.

"The boat is a lot faster than walking. It can be a bit hard to maneuver, but I can take care of it," Steve explained. "You haven't been on a boat before, have you?" he asked Alex. "Nope. I only go to the river for fishing," she replied. "Well, the ride might be a bit bumpy, and there will be a lot of water splashing around. It'll be fun." Alex believed Steve. So off they went.

It was surprising to Alex how fast the boat was. It didn't take them much time to cross the desert as they soared through the waters. It wasn't as bad as she expected. Soon, the stream ended in a deep jungle biome. Taking the stream offset their path somewhat, but it wasn't the end of the world. Steve was responsible enough to bring a compass, and they had no problem finding the correct path.

Even though the jungle biome was quite pretty, it was hard to navigate with all the bushes and vines. But there was another thing going for Alex. "Steve, look at those. They are cocoa beans!" Alex exclaimed. "You can make delicious cookies with them!" She was quite excited. Steve wasn't very interested, but he understood why Alex was so happy. She then chopped up a jungle tree and harvested some beans to make some cookies later when she got home. She put those in the special spot in her inventory so that they stay extra safe.

They were making quick progress, but time was against them. Soon, it was late noon or evening. And a night in the jungle was bound to be hectic. It was pretty easy to get stuck in bushes and vines. That made fighting suboptimal. And on top of all that, Steve did not have enough armor durability to fight that night. So, what they did was hide on the top of a tree.

The jungle trees were quite tall, and their thick leaves provided good cover for them to hide. Without wasting any time, they quickly climbed up the tree using the hanging vines. Steve died inside a little as he had to cower and hide inside of a tree, but he had no other choice. About 1500 blocks away from home, he had no way to repair his armor. He knew that if he fought, his armor would break quickly. And that would not be good for him. He didn't like the idea of getting swarmed by zombies when he had no armor. That just didn't sound very pleasant.

They made themselves comfortable on the top of the tree. It was actually pretty comfortable. Jungle tree leaves are not as rough as oak or birch leaves. The last time Steve had to hide in a tree, it was a birch tree. It got so itchy all night that it took all his will not to scream. Comparing that with the jungle tree, it wasn't as bad. "Here, eat something," Alex said as she placed a cake. Cake was her comfort food, and she asked Steve to have some as well. Steve ate a slice and sat there in silence. It was going to be a long, boring night.

Steve was so bored that he wished he brought a bed so he could sleep. Alex, on the other hand, was stargazing and kept saying, "The moon is soooooo pretty!" over and over again. Steve kept having mixed feelings about their position. On the one hand, he felt like a coward for hiding in the trees. But on the other hand, he felt a bit of relief that he didn't have to fight that night. He finally appreciated the peaceful atmosphere. Hey, and the stars were kind of pretty, so why not just relax a bit?

Alex literally didn't stop talking all night. She made sure to individually name each star she saw. Well, Steve didn't mind it that much. It was somewhat helping him with his boredom. Soon they saw the sun peeking over the horizon. "The stars are gone." Alex was a bit disappointed as she couldn't finish naming all the stars. Steve was relieved that they will be on their way soon.

When the sun fully rose above the horizon, the zombies started to disappear. Soon they couldn't hear any more monsters. They still checked under the tree and all the nearby shade to make sure they didn't get a surprise attack by a zombie still lurking in the shadows. But it wouldn't be a problem as long as they were nearly out of the jungle biome.

On their way out, Alex made sure to take every single cocoa bean and melon. "I will make a mega farm and bake lots and lots of cookies," she told Steve. And Steve believed her because she was already crazy about making cakes; it wouldn't be anything different. At least she could stack cookies, and they can actually act as a viable food source. Steve could almost imagine himself taking a few stacks of them whenever he goes out next time. Almost.

Chapter 5: The Village and the Villagers

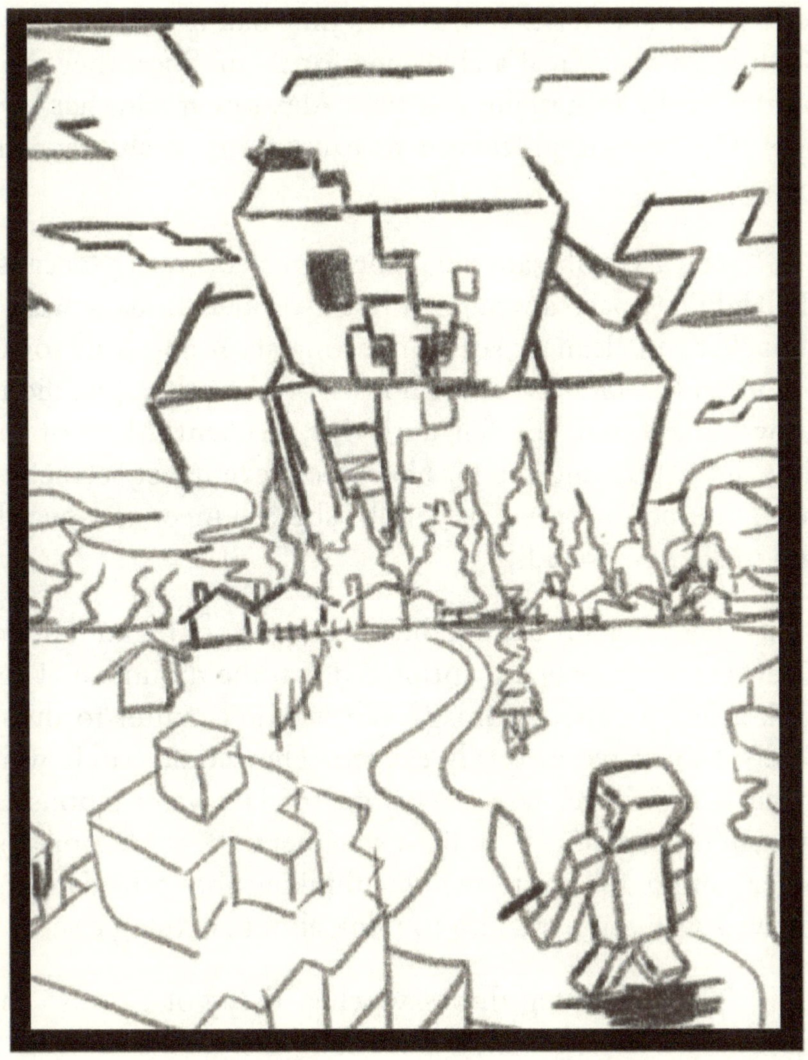

They were now pretty close to where Steve saw the village. It wouldn't be long before they reach their destination. They traveled 200 blocks and finally reached the three mountains surrounding the village. These mountains were much shorter than the ones they had to climb before. So, it wasn't much of a challenge for them. Soon they were on top of the mountain, and then Alex saw it with her own eyes. Her skepticism turned to excitement as she saw the village.

It wasn't like anything she expected, mostly because she didn't expect anything. Pretty wooden houses with a shoveled and cleaned path connecting all. A tall stone tower on one side and a few stone houses on the other. She didn't know how lonely she felt until that moment. Most of the time, it was her and the pigs because Steve never seemed to stay at home. But now, hopefully, she will meet new people and make new friends.

They quickly started their descent from the mountain. They were hurrying and sprinted down the mountain. They took a few hearts of damage, but it didn't matter to them. Both of them were equally excited. They could barely wait. Steve being Steve, was on his guard. He was cautious of everything regardless of his excitement. But Alex on the other hand didn't waste any time thinking about the dangers. She was way too hyped up to think about anything else.

The first thing they saw when they got close to the village was a huge golem. It was really big and looked to have a body made of iron. It was nothing like they had ever seen before. Steve was getting ready to fight it immediately. But it was at least a few times larger than him. It looked really sturdy, and Steve didn't know if he could defeat him or not. And then the golem turned around and looked at him.

He was sure that it would be his end. To his surprise, the golem turned around, not giving any attention to them. He was perplexed by what had happened. The golem chose not to attack them. He became extremely skeptical about it. The golem was not attacking them, but what if it's like the golem that only attacks you once you enter the village? There were too many unknowns.

"This doesn't look too good. The golems seem like trouble." Steve was really hesitant with the golems, "Should we go back? They seem dangerous. It might not be possible to defeat the golems". "The golems look pretty peaceful to me. They don't seem like the ones to attack," Alex said to Steve, trying to convince him. "It will be fine. If they were hostile, they would have already attacked us." She kept pleading with Steve to keep going. Steve finally gave in and started walking towards the village. He was still being extremely cautious of the golem.

He was keeping his eyes on the golem while Alex was running into the village. She entered the village, and the golem didn't come to attack her. Slowly, Steve followed, and sure enough, the golem didn't seem to care at all. With this happy news, they finally went deeper into the village. "See, I told you it would be fine," Alex whispered.

The houses on the edge were empty as it was noon. Most of the villagers were doing their daily activities in the center of the village. Soon the villagers saw them, and they were quite surprised. They had never seen anyone outside of their village before. But they didn't seem to be hostile about it. "Well, hello, new people!" A few of them came and greeted them. And they got to talk with each other.

Understanding the villagers was a bit tough. Their accents were different from Steve and Alex's. That's why they had to repeat quite a few times for Alex and Steve to understand. Alex was determined to talk to them, but for some reason, Steve was not that interested. They sure seemed friendly, but Steve wasn't the type to trust someone that easily. Steve was expecting them to start attacking him or something like that.

His biggest fear among all of this was what if they turned into zombies at night and attacked them. If they were caught off guard, it'd be over for them. And if the golem decided to attack them, it could single-handedly defeat both Steve and Alex. Steve soon took Alex aside and told her all of this. "Hey, you sure about this? They seem way too friendly. It is really suspicious." Steve was paranoid of the situation. "They seem fine to me," Alex replied. "You are the one who was skeptical about all this in the start. But now you are being overly optimistic, Alex." It was a bit too much for Steve's liking. She, in reply, told him, "You are being irrational, and it shouldn't be like that. We are just some visitors, and they are treating us like guests. That's all there is to it."

She also explained that she talked to some of them, and they seemed like pretty nice and honest guys. They all had specific jobs they did throughout the day. "They also told me that it would be fine if we stayed here for a couple of days. They will make the arrangements for us." She tried a lot to nullify Steve's skepticism, but he was not having any of it. He didn't discourage Alex from talking with the villagers and stuff. "Regardless, I will be on my guard until I figure some things out," he explained.

Then soon, it was sunset. The time Steve was so afraid of finally arrived. A villager came and informed them, "I have set your beds in the stone tower. It is like our guest house." Nobody lived in the tower anyway, so they could have the tower to themselves. The villager saw that Steve was a bit uneasy. "Ah, don't worry about the monsters." He then reassured Steve by telling him, "We have the golems. No monster can get past them."

The tower also had iron doors, so they should feel safe and make themselves comfortable. "There's a way to the rooftop. You guys can watch the stars there." the villager suggested. The night sky was supposedly said to get very beautiful in the village. Alex was overjoyed to be able to gaze at the stars once more, but Steve was still very suspicious of everything. But eventually, he followed Alex into the tower.

The beds were beautifully presented. They arranged pots of flowers to make it more welcoming. There was also a weird stand-type thing on the side of the wall. Steve examined it but couldn't find its purpose. There was some yellow powder and some red buds that he had never seen before. Under that, there were three glass bottles filled with water. He eventually moved away and turned his attention to a narrow corridor in the middle.

The corridor led to a tall ladder. He climbed the ladder and found a trapdoor. When he opened the trapdoor, he found the roof. Low walls surrounded the quite spacious rooftop. Alex followed him and was pleasantly surprised to see the sky. "The sky is so beautiful!" Her eyes were gleaming. The stars seem to look prettier when you aren't hiding from monsters trying to hunt you down.

Alex stayed on the rooftop to watch the stars. She told Steve that she would finish naming all of them. Steve also stayed on the roof but not for the reason you might think. The roof gave him a great view of the whole village and its surroundings. "If anything funny happens, I will notice it immediately." Steve couldn't relax. He had to make sure that they were safe.

The whole village was well lit. So, Steve knew zombies couldn't spawn there. Soon zombies and skeletons spawned outside the village, and more were coming their way. There were a bit too many of them because a lot of people were staying in the same place. This attracted more mobs. The zombies made their advances towards the village.

To his surprise, the golems actually noticed the mobs trying to enter the village. Soon it made its way over to a horde of zombies and started attacking them. The golem was stronger than what Steve had expected. It was literally killing all the zombies in one hit. It was so strong that it sent the zombies flying into the air.

The golem was quite resilient as well. The zombies swarmed around it, and it barely even flinched. This just shows how badly Steve would've lost if he attacked the golem. He was now about 99 percent sure that the golem's body was made out of solid iron. Soon another iron golem appeared that he hadn't noticed before; it was probably guarding the other side of the village. Now with two of them, the zombies didn't stand a chance.

They were a bit clunky and slow, but that didn't matter. The zombies and skeletons couldn't even put a dent in them. Steve was in awe. It was not long before that there were no zombies left. And slowly, the golems returned near the village where they previously were. They were not even halfway through the night, and there were no more zombies. The golems managed to kill all the zombies in the area.

The one thing Steve never actually thought about was how the villagers were surviving. Mostly because he thought the villagers would turn into ultra-powerful zombies and come after them, but now it made sense. The iron golems were the protectors of the village. And they were only aggressive towards hostile mobs. Steve definitely didn't want to get on their bad side now.

Lost in his thoughts, Steve didn't notice how much time had passed. It was almost dawn. Alex was still talking to herself and staring at the sky. She probably didn't even notice what was going on. Well, it wasn't anything new. Alex gets distracted by things quite easily. It is actually good for Steve to have someone as optimistic as Alex. He would probably not have done the things he did if not for Alex pressuring him. He was annoyed, but at the same time, quite grateful to have her by his side.

Soon it was morning, and the villagers came out of their houses. This time, Steve thought about talking with them. Just to know what's up with this village and what they usually do, and most importantly, he wanted to ask about those iron golems. He was so fascinated by these giants. They looked so peaceful but were so strong at the same time. He eventually made his way down the ladder.

The beds were untouched as none of them slept at night. The light was coming through the glass windows on both sides of the wall. In the night light, the tower looked rugged like a dungeon, but now it looks quite nice. The sunflowers added a nice touch to the room. And that weird stand-like thing was still there on the walls. He would ask about it to the villagers as well, later.

He made his way out of the tower. He saw a few villagers working at the farm and decided to go and talk to them. The villagers indeed had a quite heavy accent. It was quite difficult for him to understand what they were saying.

After repeating the same thing about five times, he finally understood.

The village had several professions of villagers who worked in order to maintain the village. They had tasks, from maintaining a farm to making weapons and tools. The tasks were so simple that one villager could do everything on his own. This would leave the other villagers with no work, and they would get bored out of their minds. That is why there were also some uncommon professions like a cartographer. It didn't make sense what the villagers would do with maps when they don't leave their village in the first place.

There were also librarians, which Steve found quite lame. He was only interested in the weaponsmith. So, he asked, "Where does the weaponsmith live?" It turned out that the weaponsmith lived in those stone houses near the edge of the village. They tend not to come out much because most of the time, they were busy in their furnaces smelting iron or crafting swords and shields. They didn't usually have any business outside unless a villager came to chat with them or something.

Chapter 6: The Weaponsmith!

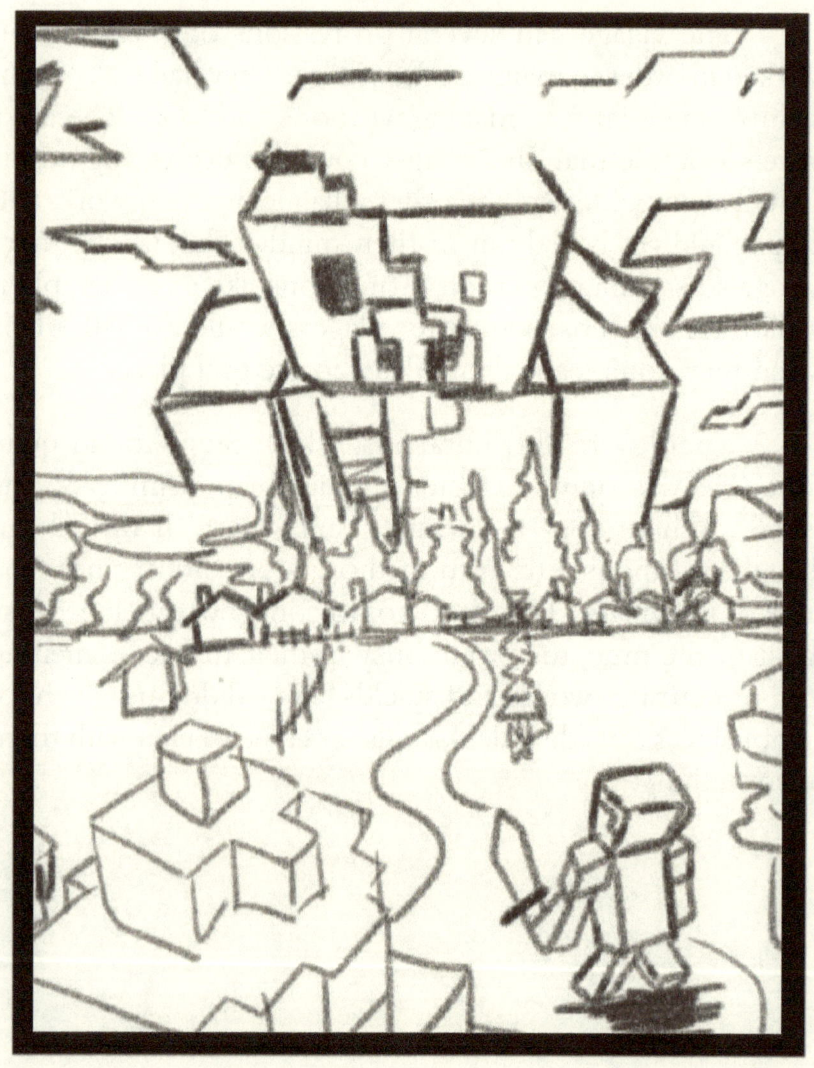

Steve finished talking with the farmers and started walking towards one of the stone houses on the edge of the village. He soon reached there. The stone house had two big furnaces on the outside. There was a grindstone in front of it. Steve didn't know what it did, but was fascinated by all these. Steve saw some iron bars covering a small pool. He got closer and found out it was filled with lava.

Steve had only seen lava twice before. Once when he was on a mountain, and the other time was when he went too deep into a cave searching for diamonds. Those things light everything on fire. Steve did not have a fun time when he accidentally fell into lava before. He was lucky that there was a waterfall nearby to cool his feet off. He hated lava like nothing else in the entire overworld. He would rather have his inventory filled with cakes than fall into the lava again, and that says a lot.

The weaponsmith didn't seem to be inside the house. Steve called for him and peeked into the house, but there was nothing. No signs of the weaponsmith. Steve thought that the weaponsmith might have gone somewhere and waited. He got bored quickly. He noticed that the door was open. Soon, curiosity took over him, and he opened the door. He thought that he would just see how the inside of the house looked.

After taking a few steps, he noticed a long corridor with two small glass windows. And at the end of the corridor was a crafting table. He walked towards it and noticed there was a wide space on the left side of the crafting table. There was a bed and a chest next to it. On the other side of the wall were three blast furnaces that were still burning. While he was examining what was inside the furnaces, he heard sounds near the door. The weaponsmith was back from where he went before,

Steve sprinted through the corridor just to crash into the weaponsmith near the end. He started apologizing. "I am really sorry! I didn't mean to snoop around your house." He explained how he was waiting for him and was bored and how he went inside the house out of curiosity. "I wasn't stealing anything, I promise! I just wanted to talk to you."

The weaponsmith was a bit annoyed but understood the situation. "It's extremely rude to just barge into someone's place. Ya seem like a good guy, so I believe that ya." Steve apologized again. The weaponsmith told him again, "It's fine ya made a mistake. Don't do it again." Steve promised he wouldn't. After all this, Steve introduced himself. "I am Steve! I love adventuring and killing mobs. I also really love weapons! I heard you make them. Can you show me some?" The weaponsmith told Steve that he was a bit busy and would talk to Steve later. But Steve was already bored out of his mind. "Let me help you with whatever you are doing. I don't have anything to do anyway."

It turned out that the weaponsmith was in charge of the iron golems. The golems, as Steve guessed, were made out of iron. Every night, the golems fend off any monsters that come near the village. While doing this, they get damaged. So the weaponsmith's job is to repair and heal the golems. "Ye could heal them by feeding them ingots of iron. They love it", the weaponsmith told Steve. And that was why he wasn't at his home. He went to heal the golems but ran out of irons. So he came back to smelt some more and take it to them.

That night was especially rough for the golems. For some reason, there were more mobs, and the golems took a lot of damage. So, the usual amount of iron wasn't enough to fully heal them. Steve was more and more fascinated as he learned more about these golems. He then asked the weaponsmith, "Where did you find them? Are they your pets?". "They have been here since we were here. They never left and were there from the beginning", answered the weaponsmith. They were like their protector, only fending off the monsters. They weren't aggressive towards anyone else unless someone hit them. Then they naturally assume that person as their enemy. The whole village found this the hard way.

It was a day like any other. The toolsmith and the weaponsmith were both responsible for each of the two golems. It was quite an easy night for them, and they were damaged very slightly. The weaponsmith gave half of his iron to the toolsmith to heal the other golem. They slowly fed the golems as chewing the iron took some time. The weaponsmith had a pickaxe in his other hand. As he was feeding the golem, he accidentally hit it. The golem immediately stopped eating and attacked the toolsmith. The toolsmith was caught off guard. It did not end well for him.

He got hit several times and got really low on health, but he somehow managed to survive. From then on, the weaponsmith took responsibility for both the golems, and the toolsmith shifted his house to the other side of the village.

The weaponsmith advised Steve, "Never try to look like a tough guy and fight the golems. They will bash you and throw you up in the air." They could actually throw you so high that you take about seven hearts of fall damage just from that. It would be foolish to even try to take one down. After hearing all of this, Steve gained massive respect for the iron golems. He realized how bad things could've ended if he had taken the wrong decision by fighting the golems.

As Steve promised to help the weaponsmith, he gave Steve 7 pieces of iron. "Feed 'em to the golems," the weaponsmith told Steve. Steve noticed that the irons smelted tremendously fast. It was unusual—another thing for Steve to ask the weaponsmith. But first, he must feed the iron golem.

He carefully went up to the golem. The golem stared into his eyes. It was a bit intimidating to him as the golem could easily take him down. He slowly gave the iron pieces to the golem. He also made sure to keep his other hand empty to not end up like the toolsmith. The golem's body started to fix itself as it took the iron. Soon he was as good as new.

Then the golem did something that Steve didn't expect at all. The golem held out a flower to Steve. It was a poppy. Steve was taken aback by this. He didn't know whether he should take it or not. The golem kept gesturing at him. Eventually, he took the poppy, and the golem turned around and kept wandering like usual. It was very weird and amazing at the same time. A mob that could finish off Steve in one hit chose to give him a flower as appreciation for helping it. That is when Steve figured out that these golems were truly a peaceful mob.

After feeding the golems, Steve followed the weaponsmith back to his house. The weaponsmith offered to give Steve a proper house tour. Steve couldn't get a proper look inside the house as he didn't get much time. The weaponsmith told Steve about everything in his house. The lava was there if he ever needed to smelt a ton of iron at once. Lava burns hotter than coal and could smelt more iron. Steve was surprised to find a new type of furnace, the blast furnace. "This furnace is quite handy to smelt ores. They burn really hot. Ye can't cook anything cuz they burn up in seconds." the weaponsmith further explained.

The weaponsmith also showed Steve all the weapons he crafted and tested. He showed him several iron swords in several conditions, from good to broken to the point where they were a toothpick. He also showed him some golden swords. "The swords are sharper than iron, but gold is very soft." explained the weaponsmith. So, even though they were better, they wouldn't really last long. A few hits and they'd be completely useless.

The weaponsmith had several bows, but most of their strings were torn. He also had several broken shields with arrows piercing through them. "The bows are pretty weak for my taste. You handle them a bit roughly, and the strings break. It's a huge nuisance." Steve told him. Steve had made over eight bows, and his current one was also pretty worn down. The weaponsmith showed him a better alternative to the bow. It was a crossbow.

It was way heavier and stronger than a bow. It was bigger as well. Instead of stretching the string and holding it in a bow, you can just hook it here. Then you can put an arrow in the well and press the release. It shot faster and farther, and overall, packed more punch.

"Ya see, I used to be an ecstatic lad like ye. I traveled the far lands and got my stuff for the things I made. I wish I could still do it if not for that wretched skeleton! Curse him." A skeleton once shot him in his eye, which left him half-blind. He now wore a leather eyepatch over it. From then on, he couldn't fight the mobs properly. He would aim his bow, but all his arrows would miss. He would swing his sword, but it would miss everything completely. And slowly, he stopped adventuring as it was too risky for him.

Steve finally found someone who was like him, someone who loves adventures and all that stuff. He could talk all day about these; caves and mountains and monsters and the weird things he found, and it kept going. The weaponsmith seemed equally interested in Steve and his adventures. The weaponsmith was doing his usual business but kept talking with Steve. They had a long, interesting conversation. They quite literally talked all day. It was around afternoon, and Steve wanted to check out what Alex was doing. "Oh, it's getting quite late; I have some place to go," Steve told the weaponsmith as he took his leave. But before he could leave, the weaponsmith said to him, "Come around again tomorrow. I got something that may be of your liking." Steve told him he would and left.

Chapter 7: Farmers and Their Farming Stuff

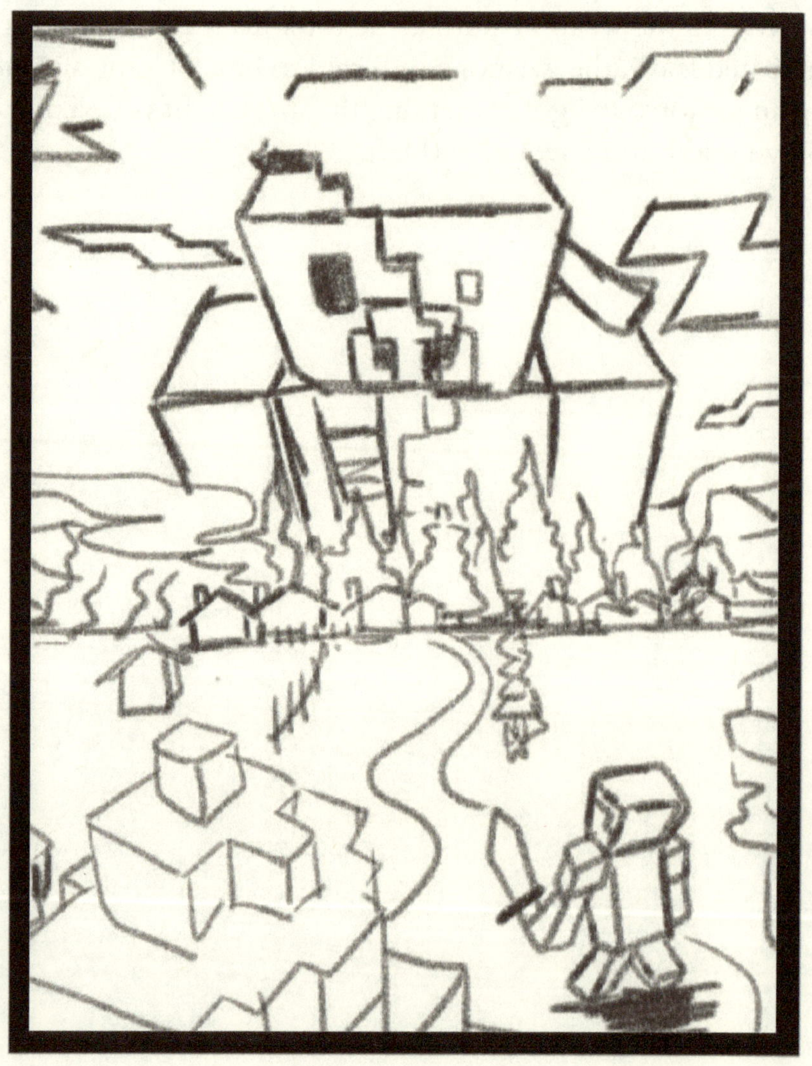

Alex was hanging out with the farmers and the cartographers in the center of the village. She talked to the farmers about how she had a massive farm, and she farmed wheat and potatoes. She then asked them, "Why are all your farms so small?" The farmers explained, "There are 5 of us here. If we all have a mega farm, we will just have too many crops. We can't possibly use them all. It would mean that a lot of crops will go to waste." Their current farms were good enough for the whole village as well as the animals. So, they weren't really interested in a mega farm.

The villagers did appreciate Alex for wanting to help, but they just didn't need it. They instead showed her new ways of farming crops. The first thing they showed her was an iron hoe. "An iron hoe is better than a stone one in every single way." Alex wasn't really into mining, so all she did was ask Steve for stones whenever her hoe broke. She thought about asking Steve to make her an iron one, but for some reason, she never did.

The villagers told her to try it out, and she did. The iron hoe was so much smoother than the stone one. She was surprised by how easy it was to till the soil. It was also sharp and lightweight. Cutting wheat felt like slicing water with a sword. It was amazing. The iron hoe was way more consistent than the stone ones she used. All the soil was uniform, and the cuts were clean. And on top of that, it was also more durable than stone hoes.

She put it on her bucket list to do when she gets back to her base. She noticed one more thing. The crops were growing at an abnormally fast rate. She was pretty confused. "How are your crops growing so fast?" she then asked the farmer. The farmer showed her this white mush. "This is why it's called a bone meal."

The bone meal was normally made from bones. That's where the name came from. They used it on planted crops, and the crops would grow super fast. Usually, you need to fight skeletons at night and collect their bones. Then you'd have to use a crafting table and make bone meal. Now the farmers weren't the type of villagers who would go out at night and fight skeletons. Forget about fighting; they didn't even know how to properly swing a sword. So they found a different way to make a bone meal.

You see, the farmers were quite smart. They found out that you could get bone meal from them if you compost the crops and other things you didn't need. It was simple. Fill the composter with all the extra crops you have and wait a bit, and boom, bone meal without actually needing any bones.

Alex's mind kept getting blown every time they told her something new. She didn't expect the villagers to be so efficient and smart. She didn't even know about a bone meal, and the villagers had already figured out how to make it without actually needing any bones. She just kept noting this and that down in her mind. She would try out all of them once she returned to her home.

Alex would be able to make everything the villagers said to help her on her farm. But she didn't know how to craft a composter. Alex wasn't a big-time adventurer like Steve. She also didn't like fighting mobs and stuff. It would be easier for her to get a composter to make bone meal just like the farmers did. So she asked the farmers about it.

"We need the composter for our farms, you see. I can't really give it to you. But I might have an extra composter at my place." Alex then asked the farmer, "Would you let me borrow it?". The farmer told her, "You could trade for it, and you can keep the composter." "What do you want in return?" Alex asked. He replied, "One emerald."

The emerald was this ultra-rare green gem that the farmer seemed to be really interested in. But searching for this gem meant she had to go mining. Now Alex doesn't go mining a lot. She would just have Steve go for her. She didn't remember Steve ever mentioning a green gem. She didn't know where to find it. Caves were completely unknown to her. But she had to get that composter somehow. So she had to find a cave and go mining.

There were several reasons why Alex despised the mining industry. In the caves, it was pitch black and sludge-filled. This place was overrun with zombies and skeletons! And she never seemed to find anything useful anyway. Not to mention, there was random water that slowed you down. And if you go deep enough, you have a risk of falling into lava. Alex never went too deep into a cave, but she heard Steve talk about lava quite a bit. It would burn like crazy. The more reasons to hate caves. But this time, she might just have to go mining. "Okay then, I will bring you the emerald," Alex promised the farmer.

Alex noticed it was getting late. She searched for Steve and soon found him near the stone tower. She went up to him and asked, "Where were you all day?" Steve replied, "I was with the weaponsmith. He had this amazing new bow-like thing. It shoots arrows but better. It's a crossbow!" Alex wasn't particularly interested, but she listened to him. He also told her how the golems were also friendly. Alex talked about how she met the farmers who showed her iron hoe and bone meal. "I can farm a lot of potatoes if I get the composter. Then I will feed infinite potatoes to the pigs!" She was really excited about the bone meal. She then told him about the trade. "The farmer wanted to give me the composter but wanted an emerald in return."

"From all the times I went mining, I found it only once," Steve told her. "They are super rare, and I didn't see them again." He thought they were precious, so he just kept them in his secret chest. He didn't know what it was used for, so it just gathered dust in his chest.

Now they knew going back to the base and bringing back that emerald was not practical. It would take them a lot of time to go back to base and then come to the village again. The journey would also be very tiring, so they decided that mining in a cave was the only solution. It might take them some time, but they really didn't want to journey back to their base.

The village was surrounded by three huge mountains. Steve noticed that there was a big ravine near the mountain up north. He suggested, "Why not try searching for the emerald in the ravine first?" The ravine will have more caves in it, and it would increase their chance of finding emeralds. It was already quite late that day, so they decided they would go mining later the next day.

They went to the stone tower to sleep for the night. They didn't sleep the night before and had to sleep that night. They couldn't risk phantoms spawning on them when they go mining. Alex was already stressed out about going to a cave. But for Steve, it was just like another Tuesday.

Steve pushed the button and opened the iron door. The beds were exactly as they were left. It didn't seem like anyone entered the tower after they left. It was still a bit early for sunset. So they made their way to the rooftop to see the sunset.

There was a cold breeze. The sun was perfectly aligned between two of the mountains. As it was slowly setting, the sky turned into purple, pink, red, and orange hues. It was the most picturesque and beautiful scenery they had seen. Soon, the sun fell below the horizon, and they returned downstairs. Steve took off his armor, and they laid in their beds.

Alex was thinking about the composters, crops, and pigs. She was worried if the pigs were okay or not. "Once I get back, I will feed you all extra potatoes," she promised.

She was also thinking about the composter. She had to find emeralds to trade for it. She was really determined to get it.

Steve, on the other hand, was still thinking about the iron golem. These large mobs were so peaceful. He just couldn't stop thinking about how wrong he was about them. He also thought about the weaponsmith. He recalled all the things he said and the thing the weaponsmith wanted to show him. He thought about big swords that could kill several monsters in one hit or arrows that exploded.

Lost in their thoughts, both of them were getting drowsy. They soon fell asleep, excited about the next day.

Chapter 8: Words of the Forgotten Ages

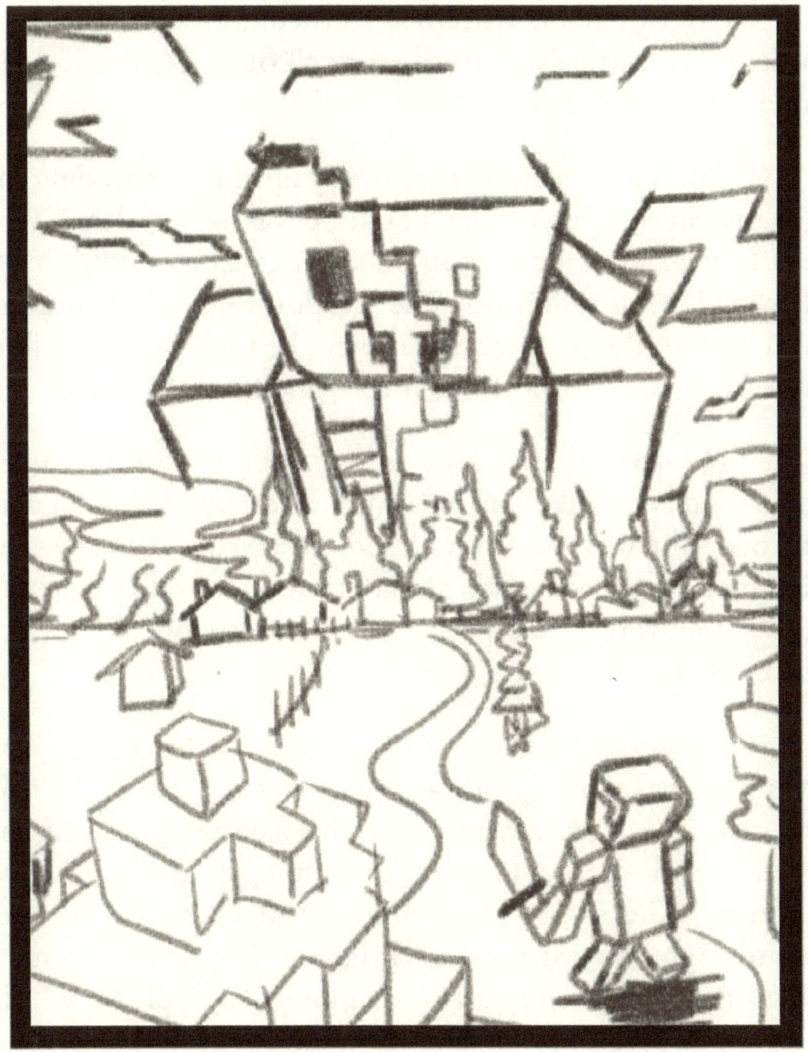

The sunlight shone through the glass window and woke Steve and Alex up. They could hear the villagers already working. They had so much to do that day. They had to go mining and find that gem and trade it with the farmer. The gem would be extremely difficult to find, but they believed in themselves. But before all of this, Steve needed to visit the weaponsmith.

The weaponsmith was already up and was feeding the golems. Steve offered to help, but he was almost done. That night, there were fewer mobs, and the golems weren't really damaged. So it didn't take the weaponsmith much time to heal both of them. After he finished, he told Steve to follow him. He walked towards his house, and Steve followed.

He opened the door to let Steve in. Steve walked inside and kept following him until he reached the chest near the bed. The weaponsmith picked up the chest and revealed that there was another chest under there. He told Steve that it was for a very special item that he once found. He opened the chest and brought out an iron sword.

Now, this iron sword was not like your normal iron sword. It was glowing purple. Steve was completely in awe. He had never seen anything like that before. It looked like an iron sword, but at the same time, it just looked so different. The sword felt sturdier than your average iron sword. "This sword feels so different. Why is that?" Steve asked the weaponsmith. The weaponsmith explained, "Ah, because ye see, it has the enchantments on it."

Enchantments were special properties that you could apply to any weapons or tools. Nobody knew when or how they came into existence. It is said that there was an ancient language spoken by villagers thousands of years ago. By chanting some phrases, they could enhance anything. For some unknown reasons, the language went extinct. But the enchantments and weapons didn't just disappear. Those villagers created a lot of enchanted weapons and tools. Some of them got buried in deep caves, and others were left in empty, abandoned structures.

A small amount of those weapons and armor fell into the hands of mobs. You could rarely find zombies and skeletons holding enchanted swords and bows. They probably picked it up from somewhere underground. This could make them about ten times stronger, but it mostly depends on the enchantments.

Usually, the enchantments bonded with the mobs if they picked it up. This meant if they died, the enchanted piece disappeared with them. But sometimes, they could drop it as well. That was how the weaponsmith got the enchanted sword.

The weaponsmith was testing his new crossbow one night. He was killing mobs as usual. Suddenly, a glint of purple caught his eyes. It was a zombie wearing a helmet and holding a glowing sword. The weaponsmith was interested in the zombie. So naturally, he shot it. He was expecting some kind of different rotten flesh to drop, but to his surprise, he got the sword instead.

The sword was in really bad shape. It was used too much. The edges were chipped, and the tip was so weak, it felt like it'd break off. The weaponsmith had to fix it. As much as he would've loved to do that, he didn't know how. He had no experience in making or repairing such weaponry. Not to mention, it was also the first time he saw something like that. He needed to know more before he could do anything with it. He then remembered the librarian.

The librarian was the most knowledgeable villager in the whole village. She had her house filled with books and was always reading something. If there was anyone who knew anything about it, it would be her, so he went to pay her a visit.

The librarian never left her home unless she had something extremely important to do. That's why it was pretty easy to find her. The weaponsmith went there, and like always, she was in her house, reading books on a lectern. She seemed to be in her own world. It sure does take a lot of effort to get to know things.

"Hello Libra." the weaponsmith greeted her and asked, "Ya know anything 'bout this purple thingy on the sword?". The librarian wasn't as surprised as the weaponsmith expected her to be. "Oh yes, I definitely do," she said in response. She then started explaining everything about an enchanted weapon and all the things about the forgotten language. "See this book? It also has an enchantment like the sword." It had the same purple glint on it.

The book was written in a completely different language. The librarian explained, "If you can find a way to fuse it with a sword, you could transfer the enchantment onto it." The weaponsmith asked her how he would do that, and to his surprise, she actually didn't know. "I don't know how you could do that. Your sword looks quite worn down. Why don't you repair it?" she suggested.

You see, enchantments weren't anything physical. It was a completely different power. So as long as the sword stays the same, the enchantments will be there. So the weaponsmith could repair the sword like any normal sword, and the enchantment would still work. The weaponsmith was delighted to hear this and thanked the librarian.

He then came back and repaired the sword, and sure enough, it was still glowing purple. Sadly, his accident happened a few days later, and he never got the chance to test the sword. So now, he was giving it to Steve to try out and tell him what it was like.

Steve was fascinated by the story and was thrilled to try the sword out. But just like the weaponsmith, he also wanted to learn more about enchantments. He thought to himself that he should visit the librarian. He always thought that reading books was quite lame, but now he got to know how amazing it was to learn new things.

He bid the weaponsmith goodbye and promised, "I will test out the sword for you." He then made his way to the librarian's place. It was not at the edge like the weaponsmith's house but was a bit far away from the center of the village. That place was eerily quiet. He knocked on the door. The librarian opened it and asked him, "Do you need anything?"

Steve replied, "Sorry to disturb you, but I want to learn a bit more about this thing called an enchantment." He told her about his conversation with the weaponsmith and the enchanted sword. She told him that she hadn't found any new information about the enchantments. "Everything the weaponsmith told you is all I know. Well, except for one thing. I have finally figured out how to combine the enchanted books with the weapons. All you need is an anvil."

"It is pretty simple. You put the book and the sword together, and you fuse them together on an anvil. Well, it seems pretty simple, but you need an insane amount of skill to combine them together. The only person who might be able to do that is the toolsmith. Only he had the required skill to fuse an enchantment".

Steve was pretty excited as he wanted to make a custom enchanted sword for himself. He asked about the book. "I don't really need them anymore," she told him. She had about five books and was willing to give them to Steve. But there was a catch. Steve had to fetch her six emeralds for each book. And finding emeralds wasn't an easy task. He also didn't know any other ways to get those books, so he made the librarian promise not to give them to anybody and that he would bring her the emerald. "Don't worry, I will keep

the book for you," she reassured him. Now he had one thing
left to do, and that is to go mining.

Chapter 9: Shiny Green Emeralds!

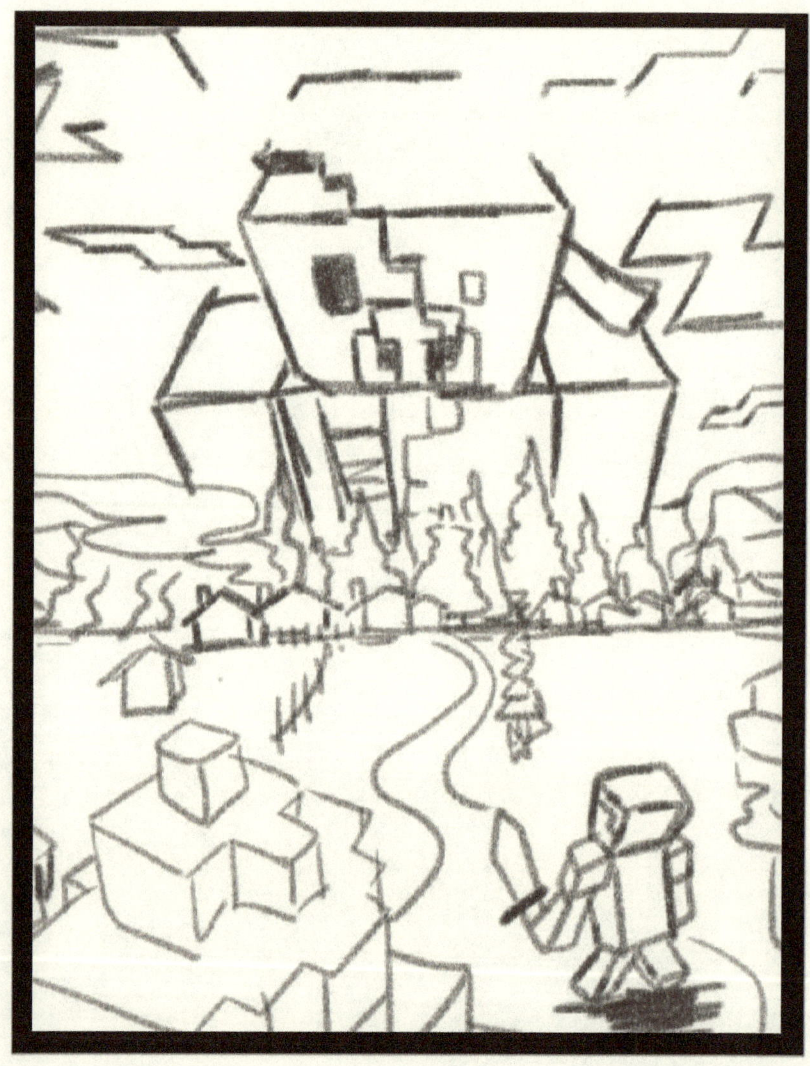

Steve was looking for Alex as she wanted to go mining as well. She wanted to get something for herself. Soon he found her where he expected her to be, near the potato farm. Alex seemed to have forgotten about emeralds. "Hey, didn't you want to go mining to get emeralds for the composter?" Steve reminded her. Alex then quickly went back to the tower to grab her bow and her iron pickaxe. Steve already had everything in the inventory. He still went back to the tower to double-check everything.

Almost everything looked okay. His new sword was razor-sharp, and the edges were immaculate. In addition, his new bow was extremely durable, and his two pickaxes also looked great. That's when his armor caught his attention. He didn't really get a chance to repair them. The helmet was so broken, and it was impossible to repair it. He then remembered the six extra iron ingots he had after feeding the golem. So, he decided to make a new helmet. After that, he had one ingot left. He then used it to repair his boots. His chest plate was still in pretty good shape, and so were his leggings. Now he felt a bit better as he didn't run the risk of his armor breaking in the middle of a fight.

Alex was really preparing herself this time. She literally went to the toolsmith and asked him to make her a new pickaxe. She promised him to give back the iron after mining. She also asked him to make her iron boots to make it easier for her to walk. She wouldn't feel every single stone poking her feet; and she also got a slightly used iron helmet, because why not? But she was still strictly using leather chest plates and leggings as iron ones are too heavy and uncomfortable.

She also emptied her inventory and put all her cakes in a chest. That's when you know she was serious about that. She neatly arranged her inventory. She took two stacks of bread instead of the cakes. She had two stacks of blocks and half a stack of wood. She also had two stacks of torches, a water bucket, and a crafting table just in case she needed it. It was the most prepared she'd ever been. She had to find emeralds. There was no way she would come back empty-handed.

Steve was quite surprised to see this kind of preparedness from Alex. She was usually the type to get distracted quite easily. It wasn't always a bad thing. You see, she had an eye for things. What you would usually miss, she'd always notice it. So it could be a big help when searching for ores. And on top of that, seeing her being this prepared also encouraged Steve even more to now find the emeralds.

They had to leave quickly as it was already noon. The caves are already trouble enough, but mining in an open ravine at night is like a hundred times worse. Zombies fall on you from nowhere, and skeletons shoot you from so high up that you can't shoot them back. So they knew that they had to leave early to avoid this. Soon enough, both of them were ready to head out.

Alex also got a good piece of advice from the toolsmith. He told her to only look in the mountain biomes. "The emeralds aren't like diamonds. You can find diamonds anywhere if you go deep enough. But emeralds will only spawn under mountain ranges," he told her. They were very special because of that. You thought diamonds were rare. Well, an emerald could be about 25 times rarer than your normal diamonds. So yeah, they'd be pretty hard to find.

They were pretty lucky to have a ravine in between two mountains. It made things easier as they would have easy access to the caves inside the mountains. This somewhat increased their chance of finding them. Both of them were hopeful that they would get enough emeralds to get what they want. Alex would have a mega potato farm, and Steve would make many glowing swords. Soon it was time to head out. They didn't have any more time to waste. They had to go down the ravine, which could be very difficult to do. So they had to keep a bit of time in their hands just in case. Alex was looking prepared with her new shiny boots. Steve looked ready with his glowing sword in his hand. "You all prepared?" he asked Alex. "Couldn't be more ready." She seemed really confident. And so they started making their way towards the ravine.

It wasn't really that far away. It was at the base of the mountains on the left of the village. They reached there in no time. And then it was time to make their descent. It looked like nobody had gone into the ravine before. Filled with muck and long vines, the ravine looked pretty eerie.

There was a damp smell of wet stones. "That looks horrible," Alex complained.

All of those were nothing new to Steve, but Alex looked a bit intimidated by the ravine.

The vines were pretty helpful. They slowly climbed down the vines, and then when they were low enough, they jumped into the water at the bottom of the ravine. They were pretty lucky that they didn't have to go down block by block, mining and placing one. It could've been like building a downwards stairs, which might sound easy but is everything except that. Thankfully, they didn't have to go through that tedious process.

It was pretty dark at the bottom. Everything was covered in vines. Only little pockets of light were entering down there. There were many cave openings exposed in the ravine walls. The ravine itself was quite long, and it seemed like it could have a lot of ore in it. This meant that it would be quite helpful for Steve, as he could mine for irons and even diamonds if he gets lucky enough.

Alex had never been in a ravine before. She had never even gone too deep into a cave before. It was way muskier than she ever expected, and it was really dark and damp. Thankfully, she had her iron boots, or her feet would be soaking wet. The place looked extremely creepy, and there were only a few holes to get out of—big openings in the wall leading to caves. Everything was making her quite uncomfortable. She wanted to tell Steve that she couldn't stay there, but she kept reminding herself, she came mining for the composter. It was all for the sake of the potato farm and the pigs. "Haaa..." she took a heavy breath.

The holes in the ceiling weren't letting enough light through, so they placed a few torches around to check out where they landed and what was there. Immediately, they found iron. "There is a LOT of iron here," Alex said, a bit surprised. Standing there, she could count at least six veins of iron ore. "There might be even more up ahead."

Steve was excited to see so many ores. "They will come in real handy once I mine them. I can make so many tools and stuff with them." He immediately began mining. He climbed up using the blocks he had and mined the ores higher up on the wall while Alex was mining the ores that were easier to reach. It was quite surprising to them that they hadn't encountered any monsters yet. Well, it wasn't night yet, so they were not expecting much of them anyway. They still never let their guard down because you never know.

They collected quite a bit of raw iron. Alex had more than enough to pay back the toolsmith. Steve had enough to make a full new set of iron armor. He noticed some coal and went to grab that as well. "You never know when you will need torches." He then came back down because the deeper you are, the more chance you have of finding the emeralds.

They then started exploring the ravine. It was narrow but extended quite long. So they slowly started walking and placed torches as they went. They found more irons and mined them. They almost had a stack of irons now but didn't find anything else. Suddenly, Alex noticed a yellow glint from the corner of her eyes. "Hey Steve, what's that in the corner?" she asked. "Huh?" It turned out to be gold ore.

She had actually noticed the ore in the corner. It was pretty well hidden. Steve was impressed by her ability to notice such small things. "Wow, your eyes are quite keen. "You did a great job," he told her. Gold, on the other hand, wasn't that useful. It was just shiny, but it wasn't strong. So it was never really used in tools or weapons. Steve wasn't really interested in gold, even though it was a bit rare. But Alex was quite excited. She wanted to make a gold helmet. "I can wear it like a crown!"

They soon reached the end of the ravine. Then they realized their mistake. They fell into a middle-ish part of the ravine and made their way to one end. But now, they had to go back and then explore the other end as well. It would have saved a lot of time if they had split up, and each went in one direction. "Such a huge waste of time because of a silly mistake." Steve sighed. Well, there was no point in thinking about that now so they made their way back and towards the other side.

As they were walking, they saw quite a few spiders hanging up on the ceiling. Alex was a bit scared of them falling on her, but Steve reassured her, "It will be fine, don't worry. I can easily fend them off." It must've gotten dark outside. They started hearing a lot of noises, but most of them came from the surface. "Um, this doesn't sound too good," Alex said in a shaky voice. It wouldn't take long for the monsters to come down, but they would be pretty easy to kill as they will take fall damage. They wouldn't have much health left and would usually die from one hit. But the problems are the monsters spawning in the caves.

There were a lot of caves. Random zombies or skeletons can suddenly appear. The scariest thing was probably the creepers. They really liked to spawn in caves. They would appear in front of you, and if you couldn't get away quickly, they would explode in your face. It would not be a fun experience. Alex knew little about creepers. She knew that they were green and long and exploded when you got close to them. But Steve was the one who knew how scary creepers were.

It took them a bit of time, but they had completely searched the whole ravine and managed only to find iron and a bit of gold. There were no signs of emeralds. The sounds of the monsters were getting louder. It was definitely night by then. Being in the middle of all of that wasn't a really good idea. A creeper could drop in from nowhere. And it would take seconds for disaster to strike.

Alex was pretty scared but managed not to show it. Steve was starting to get worried as well. A lot of caves led to this ravine so all the mobs will be funneled to them. It could get pretty ugly if they didn't do anything soon. And the more time they stayed there, the more dangerous it got.

After double-checking the other end of the ravine to make sure they didn't miss anything, Steve told Alex, "We should search into the deeper caves." "But which one?" Alex asked. The problem was that there were a lot of caves, and they didn't know which one to go to first. "Let's just choose a random one," Steve suggested. Alex had other ideas. "Why not go in the ones lower to the ground. They are easier to reach and would lead deeper, don't you think?" Steve was a bit hesitant as that cave looked especially muskier, and it felt like the spiders would love to hang around there. The smell was pretty bad, but they had to do something pretty soon.

Chapter 10: The Secrets of the Ravine

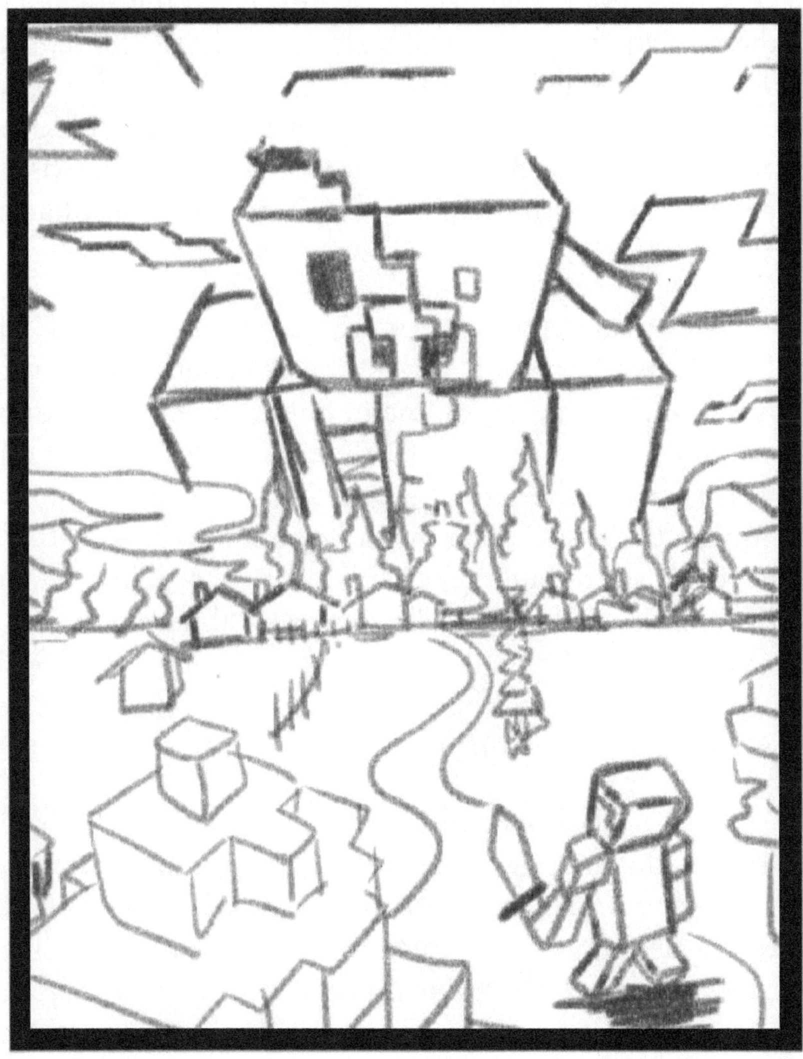

Alex's logic seemed pretty good, so they decided that they would go into that cave. "Be careful of the spiders," Steve warned Alex. She had already expected the spiders to be there. "Don't worry, I will watch my steps," she replied. "Still, be on your guard always. There is a chance that there would be a lot of spiders," said Steve. The spiders loved musky, damp caves. So usually, it wouldn't be a surprise if they ran into a few of them inside the cave. They just had to be prepared for it.

Alex sharpened her sword skills a bit, and the toolsmith gave her some advice to aim better. She went to the toolsmith at the last moment. She wouldn't even know about him if not for that carrot farmer. After hearing that she was a rookie, the farmer suggested, "Why don't you pay the toolsmith a visit? He knows a lot about caves and stuff." Alex really appreciated her advice on her going to the toolsmith. The toolsmith really knew a lot about mining. But due to some accident, he didn't go out mining anymore. It had to do something with the golems, but they didn't get enough time to talk about all that.

Alex really hoped she got more time to talk to the toolsmith. He really gave her some good tips about mining. He told her a lot about ores and pickaxes. He also told her what to look out for while mining. He gave her a brief on all the signs she needed to know that ore was there. He seemed like he really missed going to mining. He gave her lots of encouragement and told her, "Don't be afraid of the caves.

They might be filled with surprises, but that is what makes them beautiful."

Alex didn't understand the part about caves being beautiful because the one in front of her seemed pretty nasty. But she appreciated the tips the toolsmith gave her. She remembered all of them as it seemed like they could come in handy.

Steve took the lead and headed straight into the cave. It seemed like the cave was going downwards, which was a good sign. He kept leading the way, and Alex was placing torches and keeping everything lit up. The noises of the monsters were really creeping Alex out. And then, out of nowhere, a spider dropped on them.

"Aaaaaaaaah!" Alex screamed, but Steve was ready for something like this, and he struck it down with his new sword. Steve really liked the sword. It seemed way more durable and had a cleaner cut. He was impressed by how different and better it felt in his hand. He didn't have much time to think about that as more spiders were coming their way. Steve raised his sword and went in.

Alex was making sure that nothing came behind them. She used her bow to shoot the spiders on the ceiling. The spiders dropped, and Steve was ready to cut them down. The cave wasn't that wide, and it worked in their favor. Steve was able to hit multiple of them in one strike, which made it a bit easier to deal with them. A few zombies came behind them, but Alex quickly shot them and finished them off with her sword. She was really getting the hang of it.

Both of them were synergized incredibly well. Steve was the actual killing machine, and Alex was giving him backup while not getting in his way. It didn't take them much time to defeat all the mobs. The spiders left a lot of strings which Alex picked up. "I will need them for my bows," she told Steve as she picked them up. Steve kept going forward. There wouldn't be many mobs now. Soon the narrow cave split into two, one going upwards, and another seemed to lead deeper.

Now, caves are quite tricky. You can never know which way leads to where. The one that seemed to go deeper can lead to a dead-end, and the one you thought led you back to the surface could turn out to lead to diamonds. Steve knew this, but he couldn't make the decision. He asked Alex about it. "Where do you think we should go?"

Alex suggested, "Let's go into the one that seems to go deeper." but then Steve explained the confusing nature of the caves. "They may seem to lead deep, but they can also end in a dead-end. It's quite confusing". Alex herself then became unsure about what to do as well. "We could do two things." Steve proposed, "We can take a fifty-fifty gamble and choose one of the two caves, or we could split up."

Now, both the ideas had their pros and cons, and Steve and Alex knew it. If they went together and took a fifty-fifty, they might miss out on the other one, which might have emeralds. But if they chose to split up, they could cover more ground. Steve didn't have any problems with being alone, but he was worried about Alex. She seemed to hold out pretty well, but you never know what might be wrong. They had to weigh their options and make a decision.

Alex finally suggested, "Let's split up. We can go into each cave, and then we will meet back at this split. We won't miss the emeralds if we split." "Still, I am quite worried about you," Steve replied, concerned. But Alex kept saying that she would be fine and needed to learn to fend off monsters by herself. It was still a very risky idea.

Alex kept telling Steve that it would be fine and that she had her trusty bow if anything went wrong. Steve reluctantly agreed to the idea. He was very conflicted. He didn't want to miss the other cave, but at the same time, he didn't want Alex to go alone. But a decision had to be made – and so they chose to split up.

Steve let Alex go to the one that was leading upwards, and he chose the other one. He told Alex to go and see if anything looked weird, and if she felt uncomfortable, they could scratch the idea. Alex went into the tunnel a bit, and everything looked fine, or at least as fine as a cave could be. "Everything looks good," she told Steve. He nodded, went into the other cave, and so they began their journey, even deeper into the caves, but this time, both of them were alone.

Alex was feeling pretty confident. Her cave was slowly leading towards the surface, so she was pretty sure that she would run into fewer monsters. She was a bit worried about Steve. She knew he could easily handle anything that came in his way, but she still had her concerns. As for herself, she was not feeling afraid, which was very surprising, even to her. The bow in her hand made her feel powerful. She was ready to strike down anything that came in her way.

The cave Alex went into was pretty plain, which she kind of appreciated. Up ahead, she found more iron and a bit of coal, which she mined for making more torches. She was already through half a stack of torches. She then started placing the torches sparingly. She couldn't afford to waste her precious torches as she already got her lesson on what happens if you run out of torches in the dark.

Lost in her thoughts, she suddenly saw something shine around the corner. Curious, she slowly made her way towards it while being extra cautious. Suddenly, she heard the hiss of a spider behind her. She quickly turned back and looked straight into its eight glassy eyes. It was so close to her that it was literally breathing on her shoulders. She immediately jumped back and drew her sword.

Her heart was racing. "How long has it been following me?" She got a really bad jump scare from looking into its eyes; eight glossy black eyeballs that looked so empty. She had never seen the void, but if there was anything like the void, it would probably look like those eyes. The spider snared at her, and she swung her sword. That spider seemed smarter than the others. Instead of charging straight at her, it climbed up the walls. Then it dropped straight on top of her.

Alex was pretty quick on her feet. Even though she was wearing iron boots, she easily maneuvered herself away from the spider. It was then that she took her stance and began swinging it several times. As a final blow, she thrust her sword deep into the spider's body. As the spider scurried away, he left behind some strings and a slimy red ball. . "Whew. That was close," she panted.

Alex's heart was still beating out of her chest. The adrenaline made her breathe quicker. She got pretty scared by that spider coming out of nowhere. She was also a bit confused about it. Unlike the other spiders that seemed to attack them mindlessly, this one was slowly creeping up on her.

It was trying to make an ambush, which was not normal for spiders to do. And it also dodged her attacks. She was thankful that there was only one. She didn't know if she could handle a horde of them. Her confidence dwindled as she started to doubt going alone. She wished Steve was there to console her by saying that the spider was weak or something.

She then noticed that weird, red slimy ball. It seemed like this spider also dropped an unusual item. She didn't know anything about spiders. It looked pretty disgusting, and the ball was still twitching a bit. She was a bit conflicted on whether she should take it or not. It looked horrendous, and she didn't even want to go close to it, but on the other hand, it could be an ultra-rare thing that she had never heard of before. Soon she swallowed up all her disgust and picked up the thing. It looked like an eye. The spider dropped its eye.

She quickly put it into her inventory, trying to ignore it as much as she could. To distract herself from the fact that she had a spider eye in her inventory, she looked at the glow that seemed to be pretty close now. She slowly crept up to it to investigate what it was. She was anticipating an extra rare glowy ore that would get her ten composters or something like that. But it turned out it was something else.

It was your plain old, burn-through-everything lava. It was bubbling, and the noise was pretty scary. It blocked half of the way. Alex had heard Steve talk about how lava was literally the worst possible thing in existence. "If there is anything worse than having a hundred pebbles stuck in your iron boots, it is lava." He had at least said that a million times. After feeling the heat radiate from the lava, she completely believed Steve. Just getting close to it seemed to burn her face off. "This isn't looking too good," she said to herself. She had to somehow walk past it without burning herself into charcoal. She couldn't make a mistake, or she would walk straight into boiling lava.

Now Alex had the idea of turning back and look for Steve. After the incident with the spider and lava blocking her way, she could just tell him that her cave led to a dead-end, and there was nothing more than your regular iron and coal. But she knew she couldn't do that. What if there were like ten emeralds right after it? She would regret it for the rest of her life, she couldn't do it. She couldn't turn back. She had to find a way to keep going forward.

Then suddenly, she got an amazing idea. She could just mine a small tunnel through the cave wall and completely avoid the part where there was lava. "I am so smart!" she exclaimed. She felt like a genius and extremely dumb at the same time. She felt like a genius for coming up with that idea but felt pretty dumb as she hadn't thought of something this simple before, and so she got to mining.

Chapter 11: Going Deeper

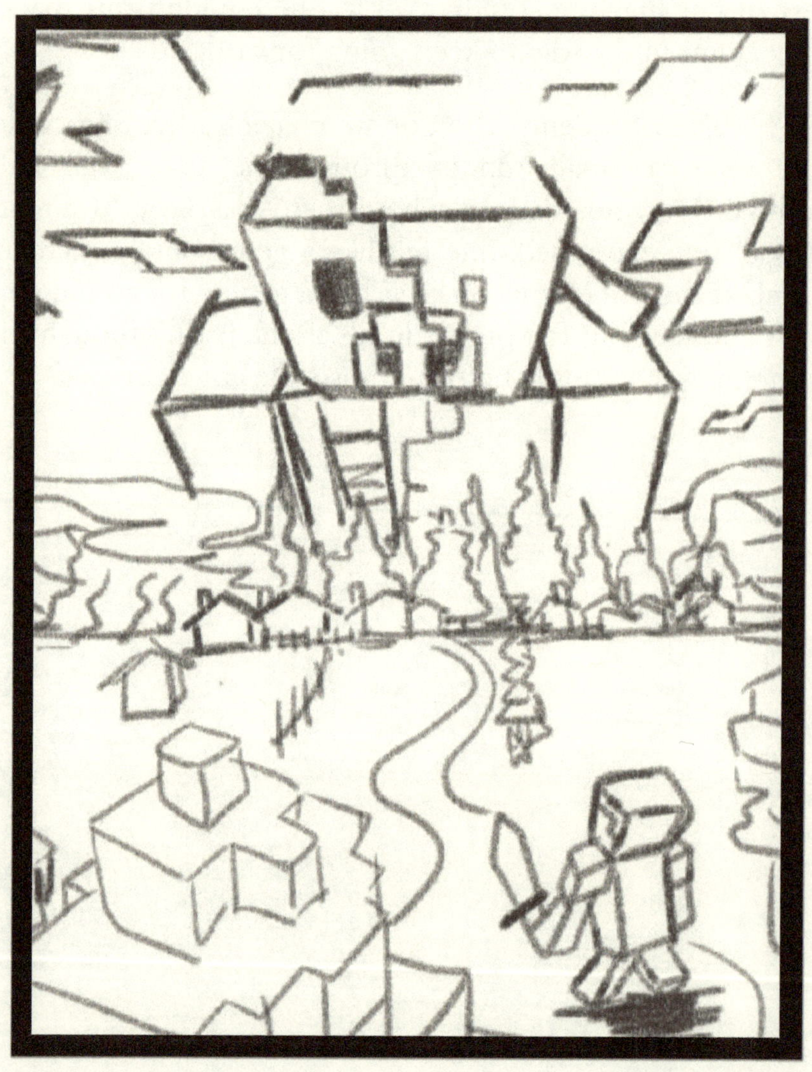

It took a bit of effort, but she started mining a three-block high, two-block wide tunnel. The stones were pretty easy to break with the iron pickaxe, and she found some iron while making the tunnel. Soon she had successfully made a tunnel and went past the lava. She felt pretty happy and proud that she had figured it out. But that happiness didn't last long. "Oh wow," she muttered. Just a few blocks ahead, she could see the cave go down. It was an extremely steep drop.

When Alex arrived at the drop, she decided to take a peek. In the depths of the cavern, it was pitch black and she couldn't see properly. The darkness gave the illusion of the drop being endless and an endless fall with no bottom to break it. "Heh, don't want to fall there." Alex shivered a bit. She didn't know if it was from the cold, damp atmosphere or from looking down the hole. She wasn't sure what to do next. She had just passed an obstacle, and now she was presented with this. She really wanted to keep going, but it just looked extremely spooky.

She had to think of something. She wished she could just drop the torches, but they would break if she threw them down. She wished there were ladders that she could climb down. She had to do something. She couldn't stop now; after all, she had committed herself to explore the cave and learning more about it. "What do I do now?" She had to figure something out quickly. After all, she promised the toolsmith that she would do so. And also, she had to find emeralds for her composter, but that was totally not the actual reason she came to the cave in the first place.

Then she remembered Steve mentioning a way of making a downward stair by mining out the walls. "It's a tedious and annoying process." Steve had told her. Alex personally never made one or saw how to make a stair by mining the wall. She had ideas on how to do it. It seemed pretty self-explanatory. You mine downwards while making a stairway. She thought to herself, how long could it possibly take? And after all, it was way better than jumping into the dark hole without knowing how deep it actually was. It seemed like a pretty good idea, so she started mining the wall while still being careful enough not to overstep. It would be about one block wide, so she had to watch out and not fall.

Steve, on the other hand, was making steady progress in his cave. He ran into a few spiders and slew them without any problems. He found lots and lots of irons. He had about two stacks of raw iron in his inventory. He kept telling himself that it was way more than he would need, but he just couldn't resist himself. He just had the urge to mine every single iron he saw on the way, but his inventory was getting full. He also found a bit of gold and mined it for Alex and told himself, "She would want it."

Steve kept moving forward, and everything was going pretty smoothly. He had yet to encounter an obstacle. His cave started off very promising, but it didn't lead as deep as he anticipated it would. Instead, it kept going straight forward. He kept walking and killing the occasional spider or zombie that appeared. "Ah, this cave isn't looking too good," he said to himself grumpily. He was getting pretty bored. He then started thinking about what Alex might be doing. Was she okay? He hoped she was. She had gotten pretty good at using the bow and the sword. She should be fine by herself.

He kept thinking about all this and got a bit distracted. And just at that moment, he heard a hiss, a creeper. He turned around and knocked it back with his sword, and quickly shot it twice in one motion. The creeper was dead, but it had gotten really close to him. If it exploded, then it would've been very bad news for Steve. His iron armor was strong, but it wasn't strong enough to tank a creeper explosion from point-blank range.

He had let his guard down. It was such a bad mistake. You never let your guard down once you enter a cave. Even if the cave looks more peaceful than a cow pasture, you can never let your guard down. And Steve ended up making such a rookie mistake. He was lucky the creeper was alone, and there were no other mobs. It kind of spooked him out how close the creeper got before he even noticed it.

He was partially blaming the cave for this. The cave was so plain and bland that he had a hard time staying focused. He had never seen a cave this bland before. It was quite surprising to him how a cave could be this boring to explore. It was just a long tunnel that turned sometimes. And there were also those occasional spiders just chilling on the ceiling, ready to drop on you. It was the complete definition of boring and annoying mixed together.

He was pretty sure that Alex's cave led back to the surface. After all, he chose the more dangerous-looking cave, and it was this bland. He wished they had chosen a different cave to go into. There were so many other caves. They were probably more interesting than the one he was in. He became a bit less concerned about Alex as she was probably fine. The cave they were in wasn't really anything special. Then, finally, he noticed something around the corner. It seemed like the cave was going downwards.

"Finally," he said with a sigh of relief. He could now go deeper and find emeralds and diamonds and all that good stuff. The cave probably wouldn't be this bland anymore if it was going deeper because the deeper the cave goes, the more dangerous it becomes. He approached the drop, quite excited. It didn't look to go as deep as he anticipated, but something was better than nothing. He cautiously jumped down, and he found something that baffled him completely. The cave was so plain that you would not even call it a cave. It looked more like someone had dug a tunnel and forgotten it there.

Meanwhile, Alex was still mining to get down. She thought about just mining straight down, but she understood how dangerous it could be. It was very tedious because she had to mine one or two blocks in front of her and one block below, which was hard to reach. Then she had to check for the drop and if there was a block underneath. And while doing all this, she had to make sure not to fall off the one block stair she was making.

"Wow, this is painfully slow." and that was probably the 10th time she had said this. Just thinking about it was annoying. She felt like she had already mined halfway down, but she wasn't sure. Soon she saw a few dangling vines. It could be her savior. She had to get just a bit lower to reach it.

Finally, she was low enough to reach the vines. She climbed down the vines, and then again, there was a drop. On the bottom, it looked like water. She had finally reached the bottom. Without thinking much, she jumped down into the pool of water. At last, she reached the floor. "Ah, wow," she gasped. She was surprised she made it.

She had no idea that a cave could go this deep. It was quite dark. She quickly placed some torches around her. The stones looked pretty weird. They looked a lot darker than usual and had a weird stripe-like pattern. She just kept getting creeped out by the cave over and over again. She was now starting to regret her decision a bit. Being alone in that situation didn't help at all. And she was through one stack of torches. She was trying to use as little as she could but still burned through them more quickly than she expected.

Chapter 12: How Deep Was Too Deep?

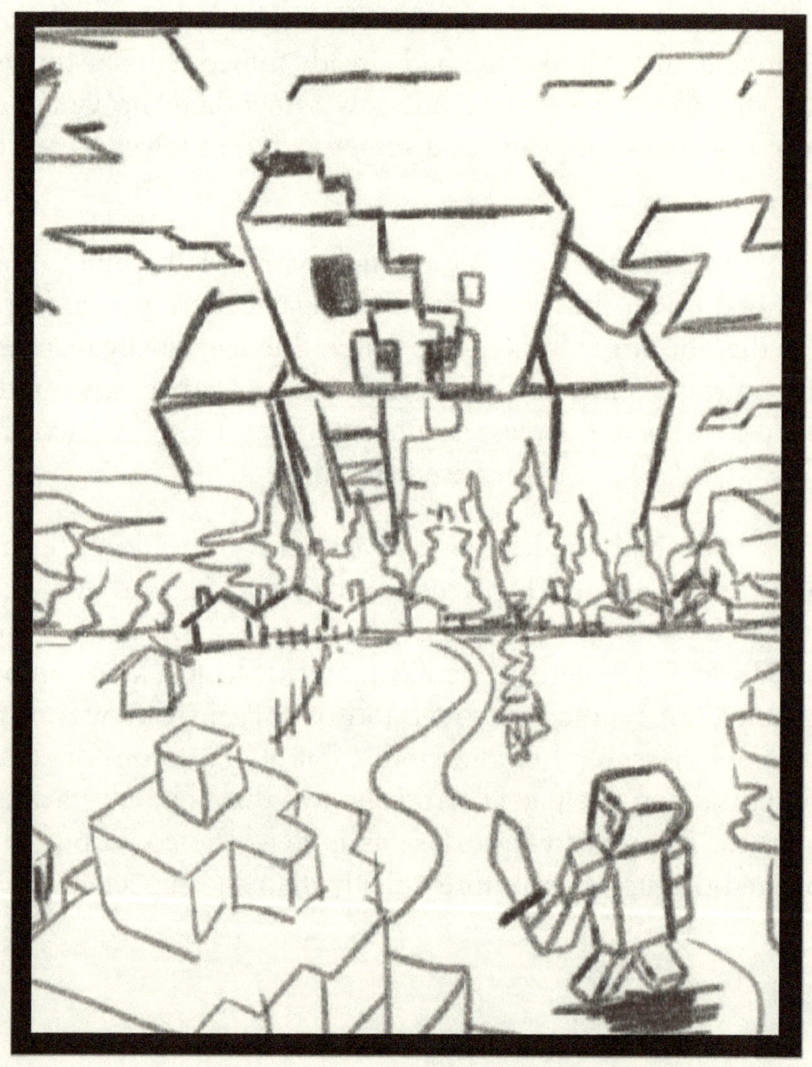

Things kept getting weirder and weirder. She didn't know what she was looking at anymore. As she kept walking, she saw some weird dark ore. It was a lot harder to mine as well. After mining, it seemed like there was raw iron inside it. It was very weird to her that there was a different type of stone. Steve had never mentioned it to her before. She was confused but still assumed that it was normal in a cave. However, things kept getting weirder.

There was what looked to be a harder type of sandstone that had coal in it. It looked so off with the coal inside it. She kept walking, quite amazed at the new things she was finding, then she suddenly stepped on something. It was a weird pointy rock. She took a better look at it, and yep, it was a weird, pointy rock. There were also some on the ceiling. She took about one heart of damage from just stepping on it, which scared her a bit. Even though she had her iron boots, it seemed dangerous to walk around like that. She had to watch her steps.

She found a lot more of those dark iron ores and kept mining until she got to one stack of raw iron. She then found a similar ore, but this time it had red in it. "A gem!" As she tried to break it, it started glowing, which freaked her out at first. But then she crouched down to take a closer look. The faint glow of the ore was quite mesmerizing. While she was observing all this, two arrows flew at her, one hitting her shoulder and the other barely missing her head. There were two skeletons somewhere. She didn't light up the cave properly. Wanting to save her torches, she did a very bad job of keeping everything lit up. Now she couldn't see where the skeletons were.

She followed where the arrows came from and took a guess. She fired a few arrows where she guessed the skeletons would be and heard the arrow hit one of them. "Aha! Found you!" She then quickly closed the gap and placed two torches. She could now clearly see them. She struck down the one close to her and shot two arrows into the one a bit farther away. Both of the skeletons disappeared and dropped some bones and arrows. "Easy."

She completely forgot about the mobs as she didn't encounter them much. She expected a lot more monsters down there as it was always dark, but to her surprise, there weren't many. Well, she was not complaining about having to deal with fewer monsters. She then turned her attention back to the ore.

She mined it, but she got a red glowing powder instead of getting a beautiful red gem as she expected. She was a bit disappointed, to say the least. She reluctantly picked it up and put it into her inventory. Her inventory was getting full. She couldn't even get rid of the stuff because she didn't know if the things she took were useful or not. She had to keep them until she made sure she wasn't throwing away ultra-rare and valuable stuff.

She was a bit overwhelmed by her surroundings. Finding new things excited her, but it also made her realize that she was really deep into the cave. That meant that it was more dangerous to be there. Just as she thought about that, she heard monsters pretty close. Four zombies and two spiders. "Oh boy, this is going to be a tough one," she told herself.

She took out her bow to get a few shots at the spiders before they came close. Thankfully, the spiders were as dumb as dirt. They kept taking those arrows straight into their bodies. Soon, both of the spiders fell. While dealing with the spiders, the zombies closed in. Alex took a trick from Steve's book. She lured them into the somewhat narrow tunnel and then swung her sword.

She was finding a rhythm. If she plunged and swung and then stepped backwards, the zombies didn't get a chance to hit her. Two of the zombies at the front fell; the two behind were the only ones left, also the spider on the ceiling. She charged this time, swinging her sword and sprinting past the zombies. She was faster than them. She managed to put a bit of distance between them and started taking shots at the spider. The spider died after one hit, and she turned her attention back to the zombie. As she was shooting arrows, her bowstring broke. It wasn't the end of the world as the zombies were quite low on health. She charged again and finished off both of them in one hit.

Alex was quite surprised by herself. She was proud of how she outmaneuvered the zombies and took care of them. She knew she had gotten better at handling the sword, and her aim with the bow had improved a lot. She was eager to show off her skills to Steve. She then turned around to continue her search for emeralds. As she turned, her arm brushed against something, a creeper. It had gotten way too close to her. How did she not notice it? It was about to blow up at any moment. She was at a loss for what to do. Her body didn't seem to be moving. She wanted to reach for her sword, but her hand felt numb. There was no way she could escape the explosion.

*****

Steve was still walking through his cave. He was killing all the zombies he could find because he was bored. The cave literally had nothing except some occasional lava and iron ores. It felt more like a chore than an adventure. After what felt like walking for a decade, the cave was finally leading downwards.

He found more irons, and the cave started twisting and turning until the cave changed color. It looked like it was getting darker ahead. At first, it didn't make sense to him how a cave that was pitch black could get even darker. It creeped him out a bit. He became quite skeptical. After inspecting a bit, it turned out the stones were actually darker than usual. It looked like black bricks, but the pattern was a bit irregular. He had ventured into so many caves, but this was the first time he saw this. He decided to name it Deepslate because it was in a deep state. For some reason, the pun sounded way funnier in his head.

Well, if it was darker, it only meant Steve needed to use more torches. Things were finally starting to get interesting. The darker cave stretched a bit and then went upwards. Just a bit ahead, Steve could hear a lot of zombies. Like a lot. It felt like a huge horde was coming towards him. Steve quickly placed some torches around him and slowly walked towards it.

He noticed something green. He got excited, thinking it was emeralds, but it turned out to be just some mossy cobblestone. Now, mossy cobblestones only form when vines grow on them. If it stays there for long enough, it fuses into the cracks. But vines never grow so deep in a cave. So, someone must've placed them there. "What is this place?" he whispered to himself.

Intrigued, Steve kept walking up to the mossy wall. The noise of the zombies got louder. He held his sword firmly in his hand. The wall led to what seemed like a huge doorway. Just as he reached it, a huge horde of zombies poured out. There were about a billion zombies in that room. Steve jumped back and began to swing his sword.

Zombies never gave Steve a hard time. They just mindlessly walk towards you. They were pretty slow and were pretty dumb. This made them pretty easy to dodge. Clearly, Steve wasn't taking any chances. There were a lot of zombies this time. He forgot the last time he had seen so many together.

He pulled out his bow to wear them off as much as he could while being at a safe distance. He kept shooting the zombies on the front and took a few of them down. Once they started getting close, he pulled out his glowing sword. With each swing, he was taking down more and more zombies. The sword was taking quick care of the zombies. Just when he thought that it was about to be over, more zombies poured out of the room. It was getting a bit problematic.

He had no idea how many zombies were left. He kept killing them, but more kept coming. He could kill a horde of zombies alone, but if they kept coming, they would soon overwhelm him.

The zombies were getting a few hits on him. It was nothing as he had iron armor, but if it kept going on, it would soon wear him down. "Just die already," he grunted. He kept fending them off and trying to back off a bit. He couldn't just turn his back and run as the zombies would keep chasing him. At the very least, the cave was assisting him in some way. The narrow cave was working to his advantage, so he thought.

At the worst possible time, a creeper showed up behind him. It was a bit far away, but it wouldn't take long before it reached Steve. He quickly pulled out his bow and started shooting arrows towards the creeper. It was a bigger threat to him than the zombies. He shot two arrows, and then he noticed a problem, a very big problem. You see, he had wasted too many arrows shooting the zombies, and now he had none left.

The creeper was approaching him, and so were the zombies. The narrow cave made it impossible for him to escape. He was sandwiched. As a last-ditch effort, he charged towards the creeper, hoping he could kill it before it could explode. But inside, he knew it wouldn't work. As he got near the creeper, it started hissing. He got two hits with his sword. It seemed possible. Then suddenly, the creeper exploded. The explosion destroyed the blocks beneath his feet. Low on health, he started to fall. It felt like it was over.

Chapter 13: Glowing White Eyes

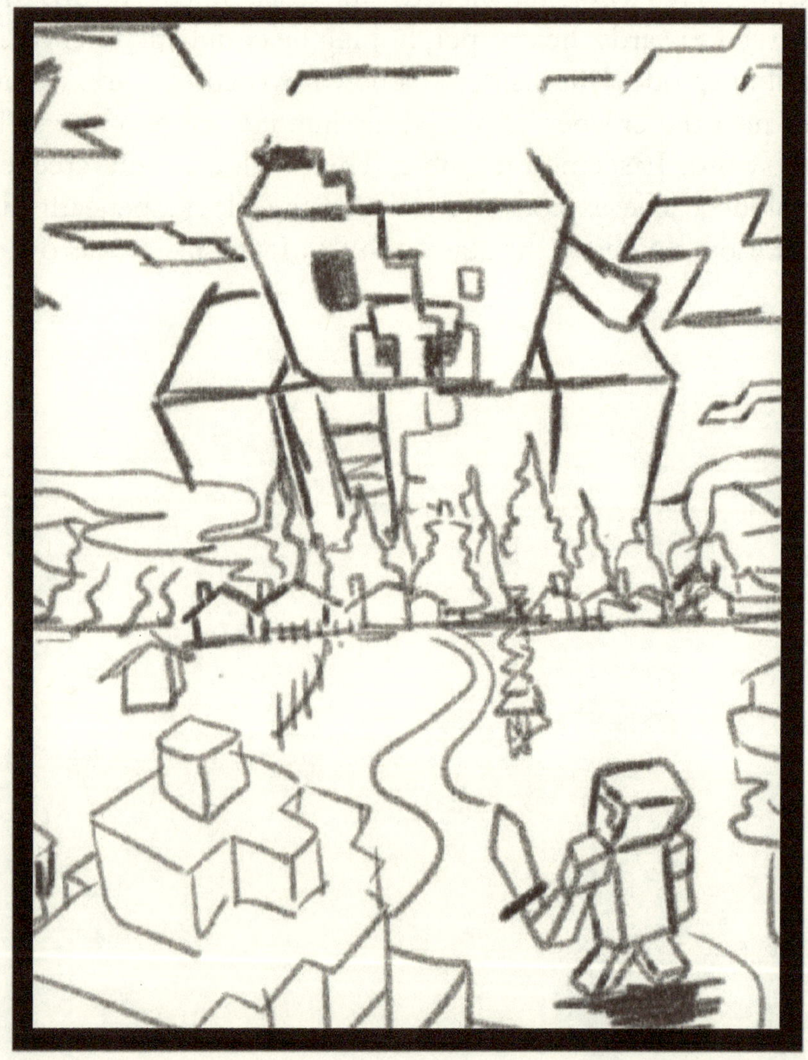

Alex still had not given up yet. She had to do whatever it took to get the emeralds for her composter. She had to think quickly as she didn't have much time. Suddenly, something came to her mind – the water bucket in her inventory.

Alex had seen Steve do a lot of crazy stuff. She remembered the first time Steve ran into a creeper. He figured out how to make a TnT to replicate the same explosion of a creeper. She had seen him do so many experiments, although he failed to negate the damage of the explosion. But one time, he got close. He tried water. If you were a bit far away from the explosion and completely submerged in water, the TnT did little to no damage.

Alex was not submerged underwater. She only had one water bucket, and she had to place it quickly. She was unsure if it would do anything at all. But all she could do was hope that it would do something. It was the only thing she could do.

She quickly pulled out her bucket and placed it near her feet. The water pushed the creeper away a bit. Suddenly, she heard an explosion from above. This startled both her and the creeper. Using this chance, Alex hit the creeper, knocking it backwards. Suddenly, someone dropped from the ceiling. It was Steve!

With him followed what felt like a billion zombies. They were just pouring out of the ceiling. Steve himself was quite surprised that he survived the fall and then noticed

Alex was there. Without wasting any time asking questions, he immediately said, "RUNNNN! Don't look back!"

Steve was down to two and a half hearts. That fall could've easily done more than four hearts of damage. If not for Alex's water bucket, it would've ended badly for him. They kept running the other way, deeper into the cave. The mobs were following them. Both were pretty low on health, and the mobs weren't giving them any chance to heal up. "We need to heal up. Find some cover." Alex told Steve, but Steve just kept telling Alex to keep running until he figured out something.

Suddenly, they heard an extremely weird swishing noise. Both of them looked back to find out that the monsters had stopped chasing them. "What just happened?" Alex asked. They were confused but didn't complain. Just as they turned around, they saw someone. "Who is that?" Alex asked. He looked quite a bit like Steve, but his back was turned towards them. They stopped running. Alex tried approaching the guy and asking him, "What are you doing here? It's really dangerous. Run this way!" Instead of responding, he just turned around.

The stranger had a face very similar to Steve's but with a lot more scars. He was the same height as Steve. They literally looked like twins, except for one thing. The stranger's eyes were completely hollow, and they were glowing a bright white.

Alex was quite creeped out and scared by this. The stranger made a weird sound, and everything turned white. "Gah!" Alex and Steve were both knocked out. When they finally got to their feet, and the white light went away, they were extremely creeped out and scared. They were back at where Steve fell from the ceiling.

The water was still there. Steve was standing right where he fell. The zombies seemed to have died somehow. There was a lot of rotten flesh on the floor. They couldn't get any time to catch their breath as they heard the noise of zombies coming from the hole in the ceiling. They quickly got themselves together and sprinted towards the other side. Alex asked Steve, "What just happened? Did you see that?" but Steve himself had no clue about anything. Finally, after putting enough distance between them and the zombies, they slowed down and ate some food to regain their health. "Let's take a break here and heal up. It seems like we have put quite a bit of distance between us and the monsters." Steve told Alex.

Both of them were exhausted after what had happened. Alex's brain felt melted. What was it all about? Why were there so many zombies chasing Steve? Who was even that glowy-eyed guy? He seemed very creepy, but it was probably him who helped them. "What is happening, Steve?" Alex asked in a shaky tone. She was quite scared. "I don't know," Steve replied in a similar tone. The way they teleported back to where they were didn't make any sense. That strange guy must've had some kind of weird power. But as quickly as he appeared, he was gone. They didn't get any chance to ask him anything, not even his name.

Alex finally asked Steve, "What on overworld were you doing with all those zombies?" "There was this weird mossy room, and I went to check it out," he replied. Steve then explained how there were infinite zombies. He also told her about the creeper and how her water saved him. "Your water really came in clutch right there. How did you end up this deep in the first place?" Steve asked her. She told him that she just followed the cave and ended up in that weird place. "There was also this creeper, and I almost got blown up." She also told him about her ingenuity and what she did with the water. Steve then told her, "It wouldn't have actually lessened the explosion. It doesn't work that way." But he was still grateful that he placed it there because he could've dropped flat onto the ground instead.

They took some rest, and their health was almost full. It was time to start moving again. Now they could just retrace the way they came and go back. But they were scared that the zombies would still lurk around. "Going back doesn't seem like a good idea," Alex said. "Yep, don't want to deal with that again," Steve agreed with her. And also, they haven't found any emeralds yet, so they decided to keep searching and go deeper into the cave.

Steve was quite intrigued by that cave as its walls were completely made up of that dark block. He asked Alex about it. "I don't know anything about this place. I just ended up here," she replied. She then remembered the red dust and the gooey red ball and showed them to Steve. As she had suspected, the gooey red thing was a spider's eye. It was quite disgusting. To her surprise, spider eyes weren't as rare as she thought. Steve had a bunch of them, but he didn't know how to use them.

She also showed him the red dust. "I expected it to be a shiny red gem but got this powder instead," Alex said, quite disappointed. Steve laughed a bit and told her, "It can be used to make a lot of advanced mechanisms." He tried to use it and was successful to some degree. It was not rare at all. Alex was even more disappointed after hearing all that, but Steve told her, "You found a new thing, so give yourself a pat on the back." He tried to console her. "Also, I have never been this deep inside a cave. So, technically you beat me in exploring the cave." This somewhat cheered her up.

They finally got up and started walking again. Alex was almost out of torches, and so was Steve. Alex used up a lot of them while making those awful stairs, and Steve just panic-placed torches when the zombies showed up. They had a total of about 25 torches. "We really need more torches," Steve said. "Don't worry; I brought wood," Alex replied.

Thankfully, she had half a stack of oak logs with her. She also brought a crafting table. She knew that if they ran out of torches, they would have to make more if they were deep in the cave. Now, coal was quite easy to find in caves. But wood? Not so much. So she brought half a stack of logs with her. She could then make them into planks and then into sticks. "You are quite smart in these ways." Steve was quite impressed, to say the least.

They placed a few torches around and placed the crafting table in the middle. Steve gave her the coals he mined while he was walking around, bored. She put the sticks and the coal together and made more torches. They had enough torches for now, but they still had to be careful. Alex had a lot of sticks, but they would eventually run out. "Don't use too many torches, Steve," Alex scolded him, "If the cave keeps getting bigger and bigger, we will need more torches." "Okay, I will try my best to not waste them." Steve made a mental note not to spam torches the next time he saw a horde of zombies.

The cave seemed to have an opening a bit farther away. Steve thought it would lead to another ravine but had doubts if ravines ever extended this deep. They approached it slowly. There was a faint light coming from the end. They eventually reached it, and their eyes widened.

The cave transformed from a wide tunnel to a huge pocket of open space. The ceiling was at least ten blocks tall, and the cave didn't even seem like a cave anymore. The most surprising part was that there was dirt and trees, most of them they didn't recognize. The cave seemed to have trapped an unknown forest inside it. Steve's jaws were hanging wide open. Alex was completely mesmerized by the cave. Could it be the beauty of the cave that the toolsmith was talking about? Because it was breathtakingly beautiful.

"Wow, what is this place?" Alex asked dreamily. "I have no clue," Steve replied. "But it is really pretty." As they started exploring it properly, things did seem a lot out of place. There were some vines that appeared to have yellow berries on them. The berries were looking really juicy and were shining a lot. Wait, no, the berries were actually glowing themselves. It was not the shine from the light of the torches. The berries themselves were giving out light. "This doesn't seem right."

Alex plucked one out and tried it. It tasted absolutely delicious! It was nothing like those red berries in the spruce forests. The red berries were sweet, but they paled in comparison to these ones. Where the red berries were firm and hard, these yellow ones were soft and a bit chewy. Alex loved the texture. She then asked Steve, "Want to give this a try? This weird berry glows and tastes pretty good." Steve took one from her and tried it. "They taste like berries but way better," Steve replied. Alex didn't expect Steve to understand the complexity of the berries anyway.

She started thinking about how she could get these vines on her farm and make lots and lots of berries. She was worried if they didn't grow outside the caves. But before that, she forgot the most important thing. It was what to name them. She asked Steve what to name them. Steve came up with the most normal, generic name anyone could give the berries. He suggested, "Why not call them glow berries because they glow in the dark?". Alex sighed. She didn't expect Steve to come up with anything except the most generic name possible. Not finding any better name for them herself, she just stuck with calling them "glow berries."

There were also these extremely pretty pink flowers. The most beautiful of all of these were the small Azalea trees. They were like normal trees but way smaller. They had leaves and pretty small flowers. There were some the size of normal oak trees, but in Alex's opinion, the small ones were prettier.

There were also these vine-like things that grew from the ground upwards. They had these leaves that looked like lily pads. Steve tried standing on one, but it seemed like the leaves were pretty weak. It wilted quite quickly. After a few minutes, it was back to normal. "Huh, weird," he whispered to himself. The cave had so many weird things that they weren't fazed by anything anymore.

They also found this very colorful green and orange ore, which Steve was extremely excited about. After carefully mining it, they got an orange-looking raw metal. It was quite shiny. Alex wanted to name it Sunstone because it looked like the sun, but then Steve mentioned, "It's not a stone, Alex. It is metal. We can't call it a stone." They went back and forth a bit and decided that they would name it later. They still had to explore more of the cave and find emeralds.

Suddenly, Steve saw something blue a bit farther away. They looked like diamonds. When he got close to it, it turned out to be some weird glowy vines that were blue. He was fooled by some random vines. Quite disappointed, Steve returned to Alex and showed her the vine. Alex chuckled a bit and told him, "Don't be disappointed. I am not even surprised that there are vines in this cave that look like diamonds. Good on you that you noticed it." There was nothing to be disappointed about. The vine just looked extremely similar. Finding diamonds was quite hard anyway.

Chapter 14: Emeralds?

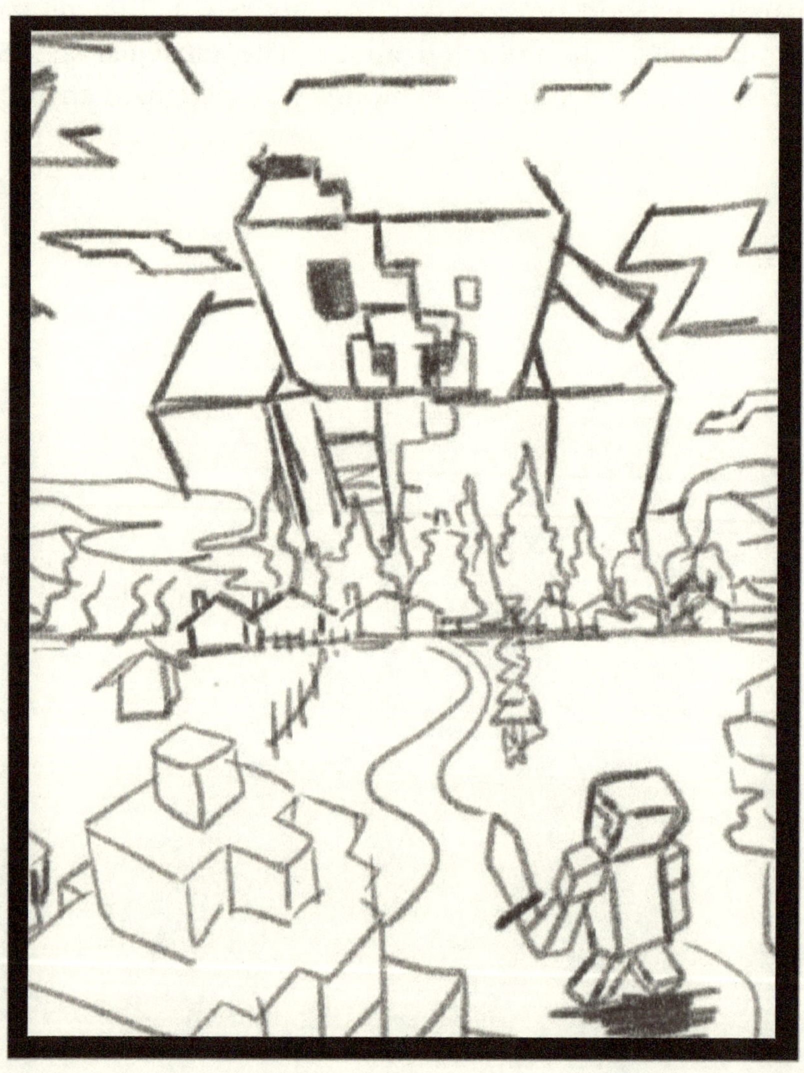

The lush cave soon came to an end, and Alex found a narrow tunnel. The tunnel led to some random lavas, and finally, she spotted a green ore. It was an emerald! Steve was still hanging out in the cave and was staring at the blue vine. Alex sprinted to him and exclaimed, "Steve! Come here! I may have found an emerald!". Steve was quite surprised that Alex could recognize an emerald ore without ever seeing one, but he had his doubts. "Where? Show me." He thought that Alex could have also gotten fooled by some glowing green vines or something.

Alex showed him this narrow tunnel leading to some lava, and a bit farther away, it seemed like there were actually two emerald ores. The lava was between him and the emeralds. He had his water bucket and poured it near the lava. The water slowly flowed and created this layer of stone on top of the lava. Alex didn't know you could do that, but it made sense. Lava is just liquid, ultra-hot stone, and when it cools, it turns back into stone. If only she knew this before, she wouldn't have had to make that tunnel around the lava before.

Soon all the lava was covered. "Now we can walk over the lava without burning ourselves," Steve told her. They slowly walked towards the ores, and Steve made sure there was no lava around the emeralds. He didn't want the emeralds to fall into the lava after mining them. It would be a disaster he didn't ever want to happen.

He carefully mined around the ore, and after seeing no signs of lava, he mined the ore. Sadly, there were only two ores. Steve kind of wished there were more emeralds there, but there weren't. Alex was more than happy that they actually found emeralds and didn't leave empty-handed. She was kind of losing hope. "Good job on finding these." Steve complimented Alex.

The emeralds were more than enough for Alex's composter but were nowhere near enough for the enchanted book. Steve needed six emeralds. They had 2, and Alex needed one for the composter. So, it left Steve with only one emerald. He needed five more. It would be easier to find more emeralds now as they knew they were at the right place.

Just to be double sure, they mined all around the tunnel. The whole place was cleared in no time. Steve then accidentally mined into another cave. The other cave seemed to be a bit wider. The tunnel was soon coming to a dead end. So, they went to the wider cave.

The cave stretched out a bit and then opened up to this huge lava lake. Now the toolsmith had told Alex, "If you see a lava lake, you might find ores there. Always explore them properly." The walls around the lava lake could have diamonds and, in some cases, emeralds. Alex told Steve, and he slowly started pouring his water bucket and creating a walkable path on top of the lava. "Hope this is worth it," Steve told Alex.

Soon they saw something on the walls. It was a diamond ore. Steve quickly went over there and mined it. Behind it were three more. It was a four ore vein. Steve was quite happy after finding all these. "This is definitely worth it." Steve giggled. But then he realized he didn't figure out one thing. How on the overworld would they get out of the cave? Mining straight up would've been an option if they were close to the surface. But Steve was sure that they were about 100 blocks deep. If they traced back where they came from, they could run into those monsters, which wouldn't be a good idea. He was hoping that the cave would lead upwards and eventually towards an exit. But he knew it wasn't always like that.

Alex was on the other side mining the wall a bit because the toolsmith suggested she do so. And she seemed to have found more emeralds. She called Steve and told him, "Come take a look at this." He heard her and headed straight towards her. Steve was getting more and more hopeful that they would get enough emeralds for all of the things. He started mining around it. It seemed to be a three ore vein. It meant he would need just two more.

As he mined the first ore, he heard the hissing of a creeper. He quickly turned back to find no one there. "Did you hear that?" he asked Alex. "Hear what?" Alex was confused. "Never mind." He turned back around to mine the second ore. But instead of finding the ores there, he saw that same stranger with glowing eyes. It was staring straight at him. "HAAAAA!" He jumped back. Just as he looked away, the strange guy disappeared. "What was that?" Steve asked Alex. "The glowy-eyed guy just appeared out of nowhere and disappeared again. You saw that right, Steve?"

Alex was really freaking out, and Steve was pretty scared as well. That was just way too creepy for both of them to handle. Steve now really just wanted to get out of the cave. But he had to mine the emeralds first.

He reached the two remaining ore and was trying to mine them quickly. Suddenly they heard an extremely loud screech. Steve kept on mining because he thought he was hearing things again. Alex was pretty scared by all that. Then they heard the screech again, but this time, that same blinding white light came back. They couldn't see anything else.

As the light was starting to fade, they slowly realized that they were falling. Both of them were falling. "What is happening?!" Alex screamed. "I don't know!" he shouted back. Steve was clueless. "Aaaaa!" Steve screamed as he fell. Then they suddenly hit the ground. Hard. Where were they? It didn't seem like the cave they were in. It took them some time to get back to their senses. Then they saw it. They somehow came back to the surface. They could see the sky and the stars. It looked beautiful, but they had their own problems. Steve was at half a heart. When he asked Alex about her health, she replied, "Also half a heart." It was extremely bad news.

It was probably in the middle of the night. They were mining away with no problems. And within the span of a few minutes, their life was in danger. Steve got extremely pale and told Alex, "Eat up and regen as much as you can. They are pretty close." But it wouldn't be enough if the monsters attacked. The noises were getting louder and louder.

Steve had to make sure of their surroundings if they got caught up in a fight. It would be incredibly difficult to fight the mobs in the state they were in. The skeletons seemed to come closer and closer to them. He peeked over the trees to find that they were on one of the mountains near the village. It was a bit of a relief as they knew where they should go. But it didn't make anything easier. They still had to climb down the mountain and reach the village.

It seemed like there were skeletons everywhere that night. Steve was trying to figure out how to get there. The mobs were getting closer to them, and he really wanted to avoid a battle. Both of them regened their health to 3 hearts, but it wasn't nearly enough. It would take three arrows for Steve and only two arrows for Alex to go down. They had to make a run for the village somehow.

Steve told Alex, "Follow where I go and run after me. We need to get to the village. It doesn't look to be too far away, but there are a lot of skeletons. Things will turn bad if we stop." She nodded in agreement, but was still really scared after what had happened. Steve started moving quickly. He jumped off two or three blocks and was making their descent very fast. It was more dangerous as he was trying to be quick to get down. Alex followed him but a bit slower. She couldn't keep up with his pace. She still tried her best while being very careful.

Just as they reached the bottom, they started sprinting towards the village as fast as they could. The skeletons immediately noticed them and started shooting towards them. There were like a million skeletons out that night. They were getting closer and closer to the village. They just had to reach near the iron golems, and they would be safe. They kept sprinting and sprinting. Countless arrows flew past their faces. They didn't lose their faith and with that strong will, they finally made it to the village. The skeletons were still following them. The iron golems seemed to appear out of nowhere, and they started taking care of the skeletons. Alex and Steve caught their breath a bit and quickly made their way towards the tower. They went inside and locked the iron door. Both of them were in really bad shape. Alex's helmet fell off somewhere. Steve's iron leggings were cracked. They wouldn't have survived if they didn't fall near the village.

It got all quiet as they slowly ate and healed up. "What just happened to us?" Alex finally whispered. They probably got teleported straight up in the skies from where they were in the cave. Alex asked him, "Why did we get teleported? What was up with that cave?" Everything was so weird to Alex. "I have been in caves so many times, but something like this never happened to me," Steve replied. So many unknowns and no answers about what happened. They slowly got into their beds and fell fast asleep. They were too tired to think about anything, but they were finally safe.

The next morning, everything felt like a weird, confusing dream. Both of them were still very confused about what had happened. Steve had probably explored a million caves, but he had never seen anything like this before. He was sad that the cave defeated him. He was sad that he couldn't mine all the emeralds. He was just overall really sad. But then Alex reassured him, "It wasn't your fault. That glowy-eyed guy was the one causing all the trouble. If he didn't mess with us, everything would've been fine."

They finally got up and started arranging their inventories. They were going through all the things they had mined. Other than the emerald and the near-death experience, their mining session went pretty well. Steve had five diamonds and two stacks of raw iron. He also picked up a stack of coal to smelt the iron. Alex had mined almost a stack of iron. She also still had the red, disgusting spider's eye and the red glowy dust. And they split up the emeralds. Alex only needed one and let Steve keep the rest. It wasn't like she needed two composters or something.

Chapter 15: When There's a Cleric, There's a Way

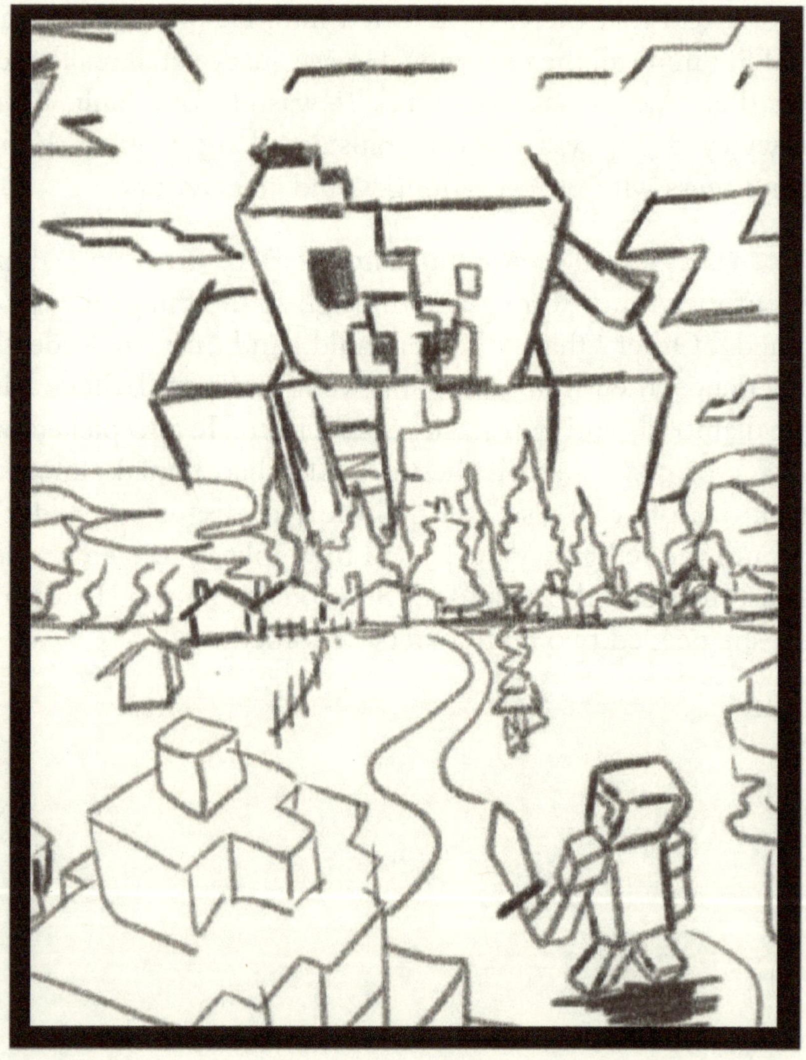

Steve didn't have enough for the book. He was four emeralds short. He could've tried bargaining with the librarian if it was like one emerald, though he didn't think it would ever work. He was still thinking of ways to get emeralds. He also had to go back to their base to take care of some stuff. He couldn't stay in the village forever.

Suddenly, he heard a knock on the door. He went and opened it. A villager was standing in front of him. It was someone they hadn't met before. He looked quite different from the farmers, and Steve doubted that he was one of them. The strange villager greeted him. Alex had already gone to the farmers to get her composter. He wondered if Alex knew that guy. The villager introduced himself. He explained, "Hi, I am the cleric. You can call me Carl."

Steve asked him, "Why would a village like this need a cleric?" The cleric laughed, "You see, it isn't as lame as you think it is."- The cleric was responsible for researching and finding out about other worldly stuff. He would make weird concoctions called potions that had various effects.

`The cleric pointed towards that weird yellow stand that Steve noticed on the first day. "You can make ultra-powerful potions using this stand," he told Steve. He also told him that the stone tower they were currently living in was actually his home. Steve apologized for taking it over and putting all his stuff here and there. "It's fine. I don't stay here most of the time." He went far away to find new things that he would try out on the brewing stand. Most of them were useless, but he thought that the new thing he found could make really useful potions.

He finally told Steve, "I heard you needed some emeralds." The cleric offered to give Steve five emeralds, but in return, he wanted something. "You see, I am currently researching how to cure a zombie. I have found some clues but need to research more. If you could offer me a stack of rotten flesh, I can take care of your emeralds."

Steve already had a lot of rotten flesh after that incident in the cave. But he was not quite sure that there would be a full-stack. And sure enough, they weren't. He was about 18 rotten flesh short. He offered the 46 rotten flesh to the cleric. "I don't have enough rotten flesh. Would you like to trade for the ones I have?" The cleric then replied, "It's fine. I need them urgently, so I guess these will do. Well, they are enough for now. Here, take these four emeralds." Steve happily traded, and he finally had enough for the book.

Since the tower was the cleric's home, Steve promised him, "We will leave very soon. Sorry for taking over your home." He kept thanking him for exchanging useless things like rotten flesh for emeralds. The cleric told him, "It's fine. You don't need to worry about moving out. I won't stay here for too long." He also told Steve to enjoy his emeralds. Steve was full of happiness. He would be able to make a purple sword himself. He immediately headed out towards the librarian's place.

On his way, he noticed Alex chatting with the farmers. The farmers were probably showing her how to use the composter. She seemed to be doing well. The fatigue that was in her in the morning wasn't there anymore. She was smiling and talking with the farmers. Steve was relieved because he was stressed if Alex would be okay after all that. But it seemed like everything was going fine.

He had his own things to worry about. He had to report to the weaponsmith how smooth the sword was. He also had to pay the toolsmith a visit. He would ask him to craft a diamond pickaxe for him. Steve could do that himself, but he still wanted to see if that pickaxe would be any different. And most importantly, he had to trade for the enchanted book.

He reached the librarian's house and knocked on her door. The librarian answered and was quite delighted to see Steve. She had already assumed that Steve came for the books. So, she asked Steve, "You brought the emeralds?" Steve replied that he had. "I want to trade for the book," he said. The librarian went inside and brought out the enchanted book. She had done a bit more research on the book after Steve had left and wanted to tell him what she found before she traded for it. She asked Steve to come in.

She told him to take a seat near the lectern. She then started explaining to Steve. "I have deciphered some of the writings. I do not understand what the writings say yet. But I can guess what the book might be used for." She was about 90% sure the book gave the unbreaking enchantment. Steve couldn't understand a thing she said, and she noticed it by taking a look at his face. So, she slowed down and started explaining it in an easier way.

She had told him before what enchantments were. But these enchantments were quite specific. There were different enchantments that made different sorts of improvements. Now, the book she had given the unbreaking enchantment to any sort of equipment. It made it so the equipment would not be damaged so much. "In other words, it simply enhanced its durability and made it so that you could use it more without breaking it," she told Steve.

Steve was finally getting what she was talking about, and he immediately asked, "Can I put it on a sword?". The librarian told him he could. He was excited to make a glowy sword. The librarian then told him another important thing. "You can put several enchantments on one piece of equipment." For instance, if he had an enchanted sword that didn't have unbreaking, he could add it. Steve wasn't sure if the weaponsmith would let him keep the sword. So, he still wanted to make a new one.

The librarian finally gave him the book, and he gave her all of his six emeralds. He was extremely happy and excited to see what he could do with the book. But first, he had to meet the weaponsmith and tell him about the sword.

The weaponsmith was outside his house. He had probably just finished feeding the iron golems. Steve went and greeted him. The weaponsmith greeted him back and asked him where he had been. "It's been over five days, man. Did ye get lost?" Steve told him that some weird things happened to them. "It's a long story, but yeah, we ran into some trouble."

The weaponsmith asked him about the sword. "You sliced some zombies with that?" Steve replied, "Yeah. It was quite amazing. Easy to handle and was quite fun to use." The weaponsmith was quite glad to hear that. Steve offered to give back the sword, but the weaponsmith declined. The weaponsmith told him, "I don't slay monsters no more. I won't get to use the sword. You keep it and keep killing the zombies."

The weaponsmith also asked him, "Did you find anything more about enchantments?" He told him about the enchanted book he traded from the librarian and how she told him about a sword having more than one enchant. The weaponsmith asked him if he wanted to add the enchantment to the sword he gave him. Steve said that he would. He quickly finished the conversation as he had to go to the toolsmith to get his pickaxe made and his sword enchanted.

The toolsmith lived at the opposite end of the village. He would have to walk across the whole village to get there. He remembered that he didn't bring that orange-ish metal with him. He wanted the toolsmith to have a look. He also wanted to bring Alex along with him and have the toolsmith make her some good tools to help her with mining and farming. So first, he went to the tower.

Inside, he found the cleric tinkering with the stand and doing something with the rotten flesh. Steve apologized for disturbing him, but the cleric didn't mind at all. He seemed like quite a nice guy. Steve quickly went up to the chest and took a few of the orange metal and some sticks. He then pulled out the iron ingots from the furnace. All of them were done smelting, and he had a bit of coal left over. He took them all out and put the coal and some of the irons in the chest. He took about half a stack with him. He double-checked his inventory, and everything was good to go. Now all he had to do was find Alex.

Alex had rushed to the farmers instantly after getting the emerald. She was super excited to get her composter. Her potato farm will be even better. She will have so many potatoes to feed the pigs. She could already picture her ultra-huge farm. She immediately headed to the central farm and found the farmers doing their usual business. It took her a bit, but she finally found the one who had offered her the trade. Alex approached him and told him, "I got the emerald!"

The farmer was delighted and told Alex that he had it at his house. "Follow me," he told her. The farmer's house was located around the central part of the village. All the farmers had their houses on the sides of the road. His house was also there. He quickly got in and retrieved the composter from one of his chests.

His house was quite small. It had only a bed, a table with a flowerpot, and his chests. He gave Alex the composter and took the emerald. Alex was thrilled to finally have a composter of her own. All her dreams of making a mega potato farm would finally be real.

She saw the farmers use the composter but still didn't fully understand how it worked. She asked the farmer about it, and he took her to a vacant farmland. There were no farmers as the seeds were just planted. They were waiting for the seeds to grow.

The composter was on the side of the tilled soil and was half full. The farmer showed Alex that any food or plant material can be used in the composter. "You can use wheat, potato, or even seeds and saplings. When the composter gets full, you will get a single bone meal. "

Chapter 16: Oh hey, it's copper

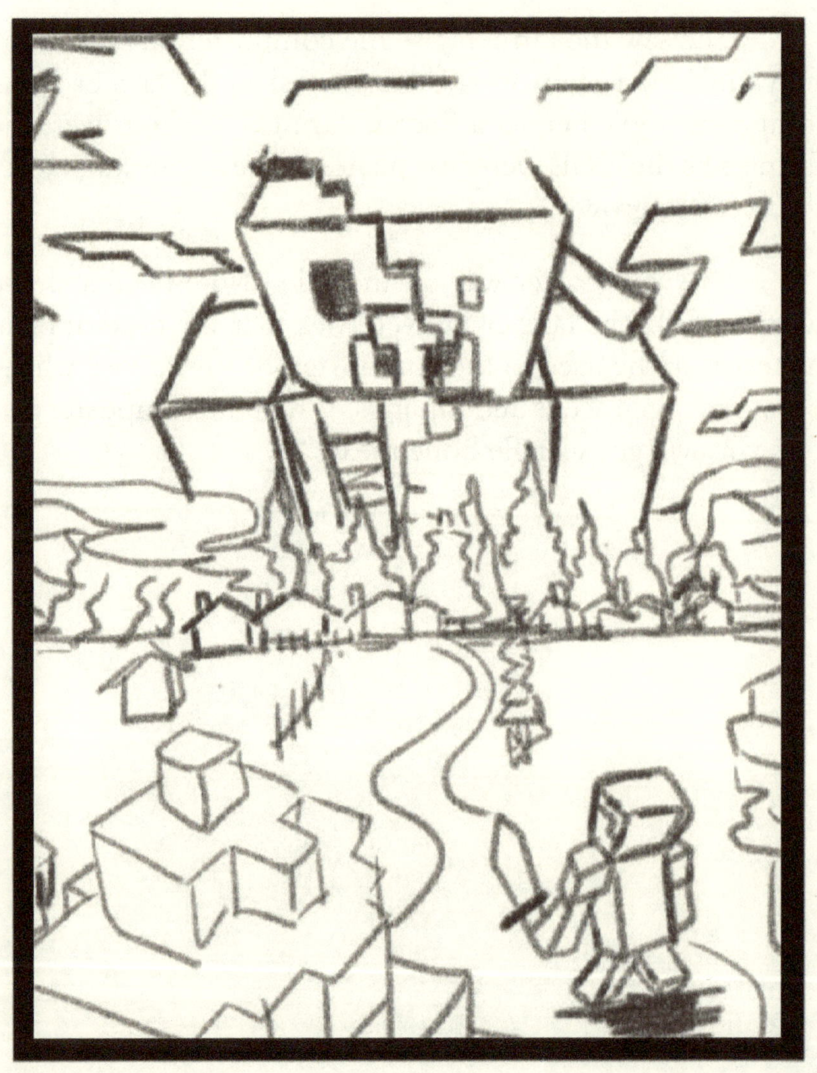

The way the composter worked was quite simple. Alex was thrilled about the farm she was about to make once she got back home. The farmer took his leave as he had important farming duties to do. Alex was walking back to the tower to store the composter. On her way, Steve shouted her name from a bit far away. "Alex!" He was telling her to come with him. So, she decided to see what Steve was up to, and then she would go to the tower.

Steve quickly ran to Alex. "Come, let's visit the toolsmith. We can get some good quality tools made," Steve proposed. Alex remembered that she had to give back the iron to the toolsmith. She told Steve to wait a bit and quickly ran to the tower to grab some iron for the toolsmith. She quickly went in and took eight iron ingots from the chest. She had to give back five ingots to the toolsmith, but she took some extra in case she wanted something else made. She quickly came back to where Steve was, and they went to the toolsmith's place.

The toolsmith was standing outside of his house, making something on the crafting table. They approached and greeted him. The toolsmith greeted them back and asked Alex, "How did your mining go?" "I actually found emeralds!" Alex replied proudly. The toolsmith was delighted by the news. Alex also offered the toolsmith those iron ingots that she borrowed, but he refused to take them. He instead offered to make an iron chest plate for Alex as she had eight of them. She gave it to him, and he started crafting it on his crafting table.

The toolsmith asked Steve how he felt about his adventure. Steve replied, "It was weird and confusing." He then told him the whole story. The toolsmith listened carefully. The toolsmith then started to tell him about this cave beyond the caves.

It was known as the deeper depths. The caves go so deep that the stones turn into deep slates. The sandstones mineralize into limestones. The previous ores also get fused into them, turning harder and more difficult to break.

Steve then told him about that beautiful flora of the cave that was so pristinely preserved. The toolsmith's eyes gleamed. "So you found it. The thing I was searching for."

The toolsmith was all into mining, but his main goal was to find the three rare structures the deeper caves had to offer; the abandoned mineshafts of the forgotten ages, the pristine lush caves, and the amethyst geode. He had found the abandoned mineshaft, but his accident stopped his adventures before he could find the other two. He had only heard rumors from past adventurers but never got to see it for himself. He was pretty proud that these two novice adventurers found something that he couldn't.

After hearing his story, Steve remembered that he had picked up a flowering azalea because he found it pretty (which was quite surprising because he didn't like flowers). He took it out of his inventory and offered it to the toolsmith. "I am sorry you couldn't see the whole scenery. But I have this flower I took from there. You never got to go there, so keep this piece of the lush cave with you."

The toolsmith got teary-eyed and took the azalea from Steve. Its beauty couldn't be compared to something on the surface of the overworld. The small flowers and the miniature tree were so pretty that they filled the toolsmith's heart. "Thank you for this kind gift." The toolsmith was on the verge of crying. All the memories of his adventures flooded him. He really missed exploring caves.

Steve also had to ask about the orange metal that Alex named sunstone. The toolsmith said, "It's called copper. I only found them once. They are kind of rare." Copper was used to making this copper rod that looked shiny, but the toolsmith didn't know its use. Luckily Steve had found a cluster of 3, so he had the perfect amount for making one. He first had to smelt it, which he did by using the toolsmith's furnace. He also asked the toolsmith to craft him a diamond pickaxe and some good iron tools for Alex. He gave him the diamond and the irons, and he started crafting all the tools while the copper smelted in the furnace.

The toolsmith crafted the diamond pickaxe for Steve and an iron hoe and shovel for Alex. He was so precise and meticulous with his crafting. The diamond pickaxe was gleaming blue while the iron tools were shining into Alex's eyes. The tools couldn't have been made more perfectly.

Meanwhile, the coppers were done smelting. The toolsmith was quick to craft the copper rod because, well, it was a rod. It was also extremely shiny and orange. Alex wanted to take it. "You can have it. I can't find a use for it." Steve let her because he knew that he wouldn't use it. "I will decorate my farm with it," she told Steve.

Soon all their work there was done. They thanked the toolsmith again and took their leave. On their way back to the tower, Steve told Alex about the cleric. "The tower is the cleric's home." Alex suggested, "We have been here for quite a bit. Let's head back to our base." Steve told her that he was thinking the same thing. They wanted to leave right away, but the sun was setting. So, they decided that they would stay there one last night and then start heading back at the break of dawn.

They made their way back to the tower. They found the cleric doing something with the stand. It was bubbling and made a sour smell. Alex and Steve both apologized to the cleric for disturbing him and told him that they would leave the next day. They didn't want to intrude on the cleric's privacy anymore. The cleric, being a really nice guy, kept telling them it was fine and that he had a lot of room in the tower. He also told them that he would sleep at the librarian's place. But they had made up their mind.

Soon it was dark, and the cleric headed to the librarian's place. Steve was getting comfortable on his bed, and Alex was looking at the copper rod. It felt cold in her hand. It tingled her fingers which was weird. Iron stuff didn't feel like that. Steve told her to sleep as they had to wake up early. She put the rod back in her inventory and went to bed as well.

Soon it was dawn. The sun rose, and they quickly got up. They didn't want to waste any time at all. They wanted to reach their base within one day and one night. They quickly packed up their chests and cleaned their inventory. Steve put on his armor and told Alex to do the same. Alex was trying to tidy up the clerics' place a bit, so it didn't look like they had left a mess. Steve quickly went to the weaponsmith's place and told him that they were leaving. The weaponsmith bid him farewell and told him, "Visit again soon. I don't mind company."

Alex was soon done with everything and went to meet Steve at the edge of the village. They then quickly started their journey towards their base. They were a bit low on food, but it shouldn't matter. They quickly sprinted between the mountains and soon entered the birch forest right at the outskirts of the village.

They were quick to get out of the birch forest and were near the jungle biome. They were making fast progress as they knew what to expect. Soon they entered the jungle biome. It was a bit trickier to navigate through but nothing too hard. They rushed through the bushes and jumped over the vines. They knew that there was a river stream nearby and that they could use a boat. They made their way to the river, but none of them had a boat. So, they had to cut down a tree and craft one. They were really fast, but the sun seemed like it was trying its hardest to catch up to them.

Soon, they finished making the boat and got ready to resume their journey. But the sun seemed to be setting as well. Darkness wouldn't be their best of friends at that time. It would be hard to navigate using the boat at night. But they had to keep moving. They didn't want to waste any time. Even if it was hard to navigate using a boat, it was much quicker than walking on foot.

They went off just as the sun fully set. Steve was rowing the boat, and Alex was holding a torch to somewhat help him see where he was going. It was a surprisingly peaceful night. They didn't hear any monsters nearby. They decided to travel at night as well because they were more confident in their combat skills. Alex had significantly improved her skills with a sword and had incredibly precise aim with a bow.

She also got her iron chest plate made by the toolsmith. It was surprisingly not as uncomfortable as she thought. It felt way sturdier and boosted her confidence even more. Steve had his trusty glowing sword. He kept his book as he didn't know whether it would be a good idea to put it on his sword or not. He would have asked the toolsmith, but he forgot about it.

They were making steady progress, and soon, the river ended. They got a nice welcome from some zombies and a skeleton. They took care of them and kept moving forward.

Soon they were in the oak forests. They were almost home. They just had to pass that. Their base was in the plains biome, which was right after the forest.

One good news was that the sun was rising. It was going to be a lot easier to navigate in daylight. They didn't stop and kept moving till they reached their base. Soon they were out of the forest, and they could see their base a bit far away. They sprinted through it and reached their base just as the sun was fully up.

Chapter 17: Home Sweet Home

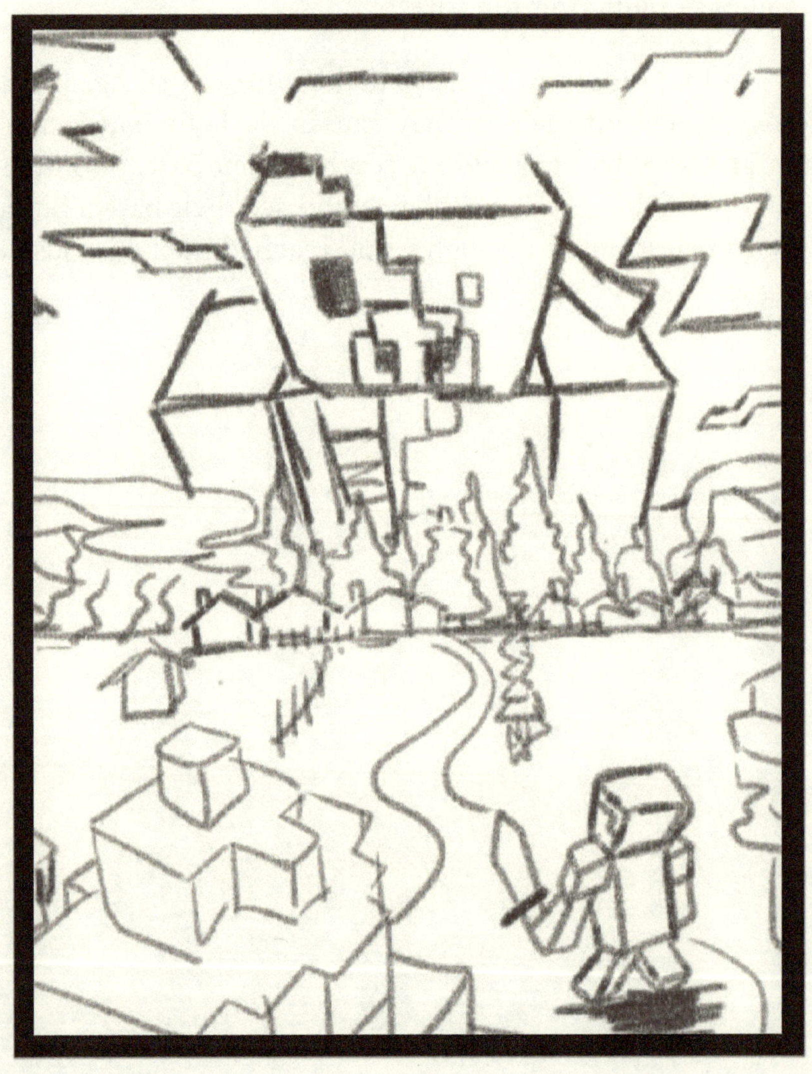

Both of them were equally surprised by how little time it took them to get back to their base. They did run through all the biomes without making any breaks. They also ignored all the mobs that didn't directly get in their way. They also realized another thing. They took a longer route to the village before. This time they literally went straight, and it wasn't really that far away. What seemed like over 2500 blocks actually turned out to be just a bit over a thousand blocks.

Steve memorized the path as they came back. It'd be easier for them to return to the village if they needed to. But for now, they were back home, and they had stuff to take care of.

Steve went to his box house and refilled the chests with the ores and stuff he found. He restocked his food supply. He always had extra but was going to run out if he didn't go hunting soon quickly. He tidied up his place a bit and went down to the basement.

The basement was where he hid his super rare and valuable stuff. He carefully stored his valuable enchanted book. He thought about storing the diamond pickaxe as well but decided to use it for a bit. He also noticed how mucky the basement had become. He opened it up a bit and decided he would clean it later. He double-checked and marked where he kept the book and left. He picked up some arrows and headed out to go hunting.

Meanwhile, Alex immediately ran up to the field in front of her house. She checked the chest she left. To no one's surprise, the pigs weren't able to open it and couldn't eat any of the potatoes. She took some of the potatoes out, and all the pigs started swarming her. She was extremely happy to see her pigs and fed them one by one. It took her a lot of time, but she fed all of them. Almost half of the chest of potato was empty when she was done. After traveling for so long and feeding the pigs, she was a little tired but still decided to work on her farm.

She added a new row of tilled soil to plant more potatoes. She harvested the ones that were fully grown and replanted them. She made sure that water was reaching all of it. And the most important part, she put the composter right in the middle. She would gather all the stuff she doesn't need and boost her potato farm. The bone meals were quite effective.

She suddenly remembered about the shiny copper rod. She didn't know where to put it. It looked really pretty, but she wished she had another one to make a gateway type of decoration. But she didn't. So, she just randomly placed it in the field where pigs hung out. Immediately the pigs noticed this and swarmed around it.

All the pigs were quite curious. When they saw this new shiny thing, they all came to see what was up with that. They were going near it and sniffing it. They all were gathering around and just hanging out around it. Alex noticed this and picked it up. She then got an idea. She could just place it when she had to feed the pigs. The pigs would come near it, and it would be easier for her to feed them together. She was a genius.

Meanwhile, Steve was getting out of his box house to get some food. He had more than he would need but still wanted to keep everything stocked up. He noticed all their paths were covered in grass. Their whole place was overgrown. Only Alex's farm and the pig's fields were spared. Now, Steve wasn't the guy who was into cleaning and stuff, but the grass infuriated him enough that he decided that he would clean their pathways.

He noticed Alex was doing something with the pigs, and they seemed to swarm around her. It wasn't anything unusual to Steve. Alex's pigs would always rush to her whenever she brought out potatoes. As he got near Alex, all the pigs started to scram. Steve's clunking iron armor most probably scared them away. He turned to Alex. She seemed quite tired. He asked, "What's up?" "I was feeding the pigs, Steve, and now you scared them away," she replied, a bit frustrated.

Steve apologized and asked her for the shovel. He offered to clean in front of her house as well, as she was surely tired after all that. Alex was quite surprised. "You are being responsible for once. That's quite rare." She gave him the shovel. "Here, take it." She was actually quite tired but had to do one last thing. She had to prepare her cocoa bean farm.

It was quite time-consuming to build a farm from scratch. But she soon got to work. While she was at the village, she got some advice from the villagers on how to build an amazing cocoa farm; It turns out you can only plant cocoa beans on jungle tree logs. It won't grow anywhere else. So the first thing she had to do was plant some of the saplings she picked up when she was in the biome. She fenced off a huge area to the left side of her potato farm and planted the saplings. She planted them in a neat row. Each sapling was the perfect distance apart to make it look uniform. Now all she had to do was wait for them to grow.

She was finally done with her tasks and went to her house to destress and relax a bit. She would sit out in front of her house and just watch the flowers and chill. It was a bit after midday, so she had a lot of time left. She planned to bake her cakes in the evening. She was going to get some rest.

Steve was done with the grass. They were itchy and tickled him through his armor. The grass had gotten way too tall. He pulled out his shovel and started shoveling the pathway they previously had. It was astonishing how much the grass grew in the last few days. It was taking Steve quite a bit of time to get rid of it. Finally, the path was clear, but he still had to remove the grass from in front of both their houses.

He took the shovel and literally started whacking the grass off of the ground. He was getting quite frustrated by the grass. Meanwhile, Alex was just sitting on her porch and watching Steve rage at some random overgrown grass. She had a good laugh. "You could use a hoe to cut it, you know. It'd be way easier." Steve asked her for it, and she gave it to him. It was obviously easier to trim the grass instead of whacking it into the ground. Steve was finally making some progress.

He eventually finished taking care of all the grass and headed towards the forest to go gather some food. Alex, having nothing else to do, returned inside her house and started baking cakes. She was running out of milk and decided to make just one. She didn't have enough energy left to go and milk the cows again.

She took one of the milk buckets and took a bit of wheat, eggs, and sugar. She then took them all and started making the cake. It turned out to be beautiful and tasted amazing. It was so perfect that she wanted to make another one. But she decided to make a cookie instead. She wanted to keep all the cocoa for the farm but decided that using only one couldn't hurt. She took two wheat and a cocoa bean and started making the cookie. It was her first time making one. She was just doing everything from her instincts as she had years and years of experience crafting cakes. After a bit, the cookie seemed to be done. It looked absolutely stunning.

The cookie itself was crispy and flaky, and the cocoa beans turned dark and silky. It didn't need any extra sugar. The cocoa gave it a slightly sweet taste with a hint of bitterness. Her tongue was getting overwhelmed with flavors and textures. She was literally having the best time of her life.

Sadly, the cookie was finished. It was quite small compared to a cake. She really wanted to make more and eat like a thousand of them. But she stopped herself. If she used up all the cocoa beans, then she wouldn't have any for the farm. She still decided to make just one more for Steve to taste. She was sure his mind would be blown after tasting it.

Steve was out far away, searching for cows and pigs to hunt. Cooked beef and pork chops were by far the most efficient and widely available food. Alex's cakes were decent but didn't have the versatility the beef and porkchop had. You could eat one of them, and almost all of your hunger bars would be full. Steve chose these because they were more practical, and you could stack them. You also don't have to place it like you need to with a cake. In his opinion, cooked beef was, by far, the most superior food.

He didn't have much pork chops these days anyway. After he found out that Alex loved pigs so much, he stopped hunting pigs. He just didn't want her to get sad knowing Steve hunted pigs. He hunted cows instead. They dropped a similar amount of food, and the saturation they provided was the same.

Steve's hunting session was pretty uneventful. He only managed to find one cow and get three pieces of raw beef. He wanted to search further, but it was getting late. He reluctantly returned back home. He was a bit disappointed as well. When he returned, he found out Alex was waiting for him. She made him a cookie. "Oh, thanks." He then took it. He was heading into his house and bit into the cookie. It was crunchy and a bit hard but had soft, silky cocoa. It tasted amazing. Well, at least it was better than the cakes. Steve really liked it. He was looking forward to Alex making unnecessarily huge amounts of cookies because he might actually eat them this time.

The next morning, Steve headed out as fast as he could. He had to gather food because he was running dangerously low. Well, he actually wasn't. He had this double chest full of food, but he refused to take them. They were only for emergencies. Now we don't get what emergency would you need a double chest filled with cooked beef, but Steve wouldn't take anything from there.

Alex was tending to her farm as her daily routine. She harvested her potatoes and replanted them. But she had a new task now. That was filling up her composter. She filled it up quite a few times and got a lot of bone meals.

It turns out that she could use the bone meals also to grow saplings. The jungle saplings she planted grew up in no time; two rows of perfectly planted jungle trees. All she had to do now was grow the cocoa beans on the logs of the jungle trees. She planted them. Now, she had to wait.

Steve was lucky that morning. He found a group of cows randomly hanging around near a small pond. He took out his bow and took quick care of them. He got a lot more beef than yesterday. It was enough to last him a week. So, he decided he would return to his house.

Meanwhile, Alex decided to feed the pigs. She put down the shiny rod, and all the pigs came rushing towards it. It made her job way easier. She was almost done when Steve called her. "You got any more of those cookies?" he asked her. Alex was quite surprised that Steve was asking for the cookies. She replied, "I don't, but I have some extra cocoa after making the farm. I'll make some more once I am done with feeding the pigs."

She was quick to feed the pigs as Steve was rarely enthusiastic about eating whatever Alex made. She quickly got into her house and took the wheat and cocoa. She showed Steve how to make them. She put the wheat and cocoa and did some things and after a bit, voila! Cookies!

Steve didn't understand how she made them so quickly. He didn't even understand how she made them in the first place. Without thinking much, he took some of the cookies and thanked Alex. Alex was pleased. "Let's go to this small hill. It's nearby, and the view is really pretty." Alex suggested. She had planted some flowers, and you could also see the sunset from there. It was a beautiful view, and eating cookies there would be amazing. Steve agreed, and they went to the hill.

It was much shorter than your average mountain because; it wasn't one. Steve quickly climbed up and saw the flowers. Alex worked quite hard planting them. "Wow, they are really beautiful. You seem to have spent quite some time working here." Steve was quite amazed. The flowers grew freely but had a beautiful pattern to them. It was late afternoon, so they had to wait a bit till sunset. Steve was munching on the cookies, and Alex was admiring her flowers.

Soon the sun was setting. It looked extremely pretty. The flower glowed with a golden hue as the sun set. Even Steve was mesmerized by how pretty it looked. Alex had quite put a bit of thought into choosing the location and how she planted the flower. Steve could never do that. He never had the eye for beauty as Alex did.

The sunset was over quickly, and they had to return to their home. The monsters would soon start spawning, and that was the last thing they wanted to deal with. They quickly made their way back to the base and went to their respective houses. Soon they got into their beds and fell asleep.

Chapter 18: Endless troubles

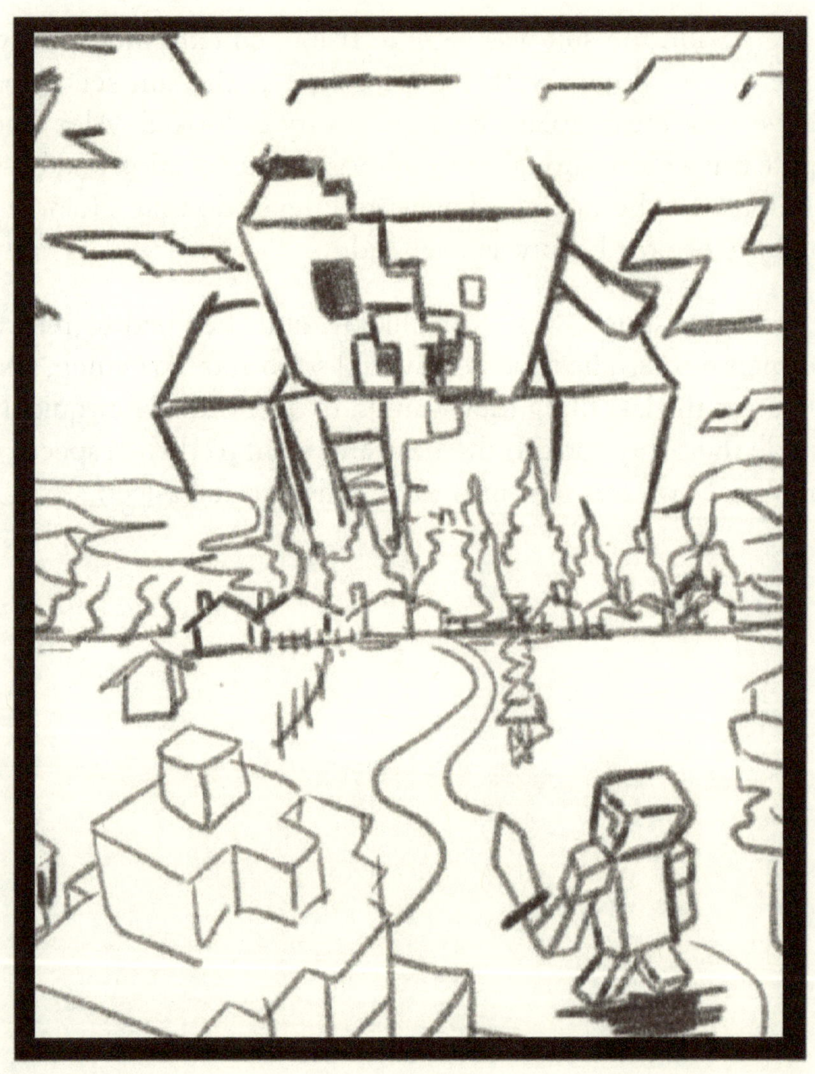

Alex woke up to the sound of thunder. It was a bit after dawn. The clouds filled the sky. The sun was completely blocked out. She couldn't even tell it was already dawn. It started to rain a little. A few drops were hitting the ground. It had been a long time since it last rained. Alex was a bit worried about her farms, but the rain usually didn't damage them. She wondered if Steve was up yet. Slowly she got to a window to check out what was happening. It was far worse than she expected.

The clouds were a hue of dark grey to the point they looked almost pitch black. It looked like night had fallen, and there wasn't a single ray of sunlight hitting the ground. This scared her a bit. She should be fine as long as she is in her house. The rain started to pour harder. It made quite a bit of noise on her wooden roof. Suddenly, she heard another loud thunder. The rain was turning into a full-fledged thunderstorm. She had expected it after seeing the clouds.

Steve woke up a bit later and was not really happy to see the rain. He was annoyed that he couldn't get out and do stuff. He wasn't really sure what he would do, but he couldn't, and that's what annoyed him. "I hate this rain!" he screamed. He put on his armor, took it off, then put it on again. He was bored, like really bored. The sound of rain was obnoxious, and the loud thunder was straight-up scary. He hated the fact that if he ran out in the rain, there was a small chance of him getting struck by lightning. He was really uncomfortable knowing that there is a chance of that happening, no matter how small it was.

He eventually decided that it would be better to hang out at Alex's place than sit in his house alone. He put on his iron helmet so that his head wouldn't get wet. Then he got out of his house and ran as fast as he could.

Alex was sitting near the window, looking at the rain fall. Suddenly, her door burst open. She jumped up. "WHAAAA?!" she shrieked. It was Steve, soaking wet. She was mad at him. "You gave me such a jump scare, Steve! Why are you here?" she said to him angrily. She was already stressed due to the rain. Steve apologized and said, "I was bored. So, I came here." Alex told him, "At least knock or open the door like a normal person and don't ram it like a horde of zombies is breaking into my house. My heart almost jumped out of my chest."

Alex ranted for a bit, but she eventually cooled down. Alex could never hold her anger which was a good thing. They then started talking about random things. The thunder was getting louder and louder. Alex was starting to get really worried. Then she remembered her pigs! She totally forgot to check on them. She told that to Steve, and they quickly went to the back of the house. It started raining even heavier. The lightning started striking left, right, and center. When they peeked out of the window, Alex was in shock after what she saw.

Eight of her pigs were standing near that weird rod she placed. They probably didn't leave as she forgot to pick it up after she was done feeding them. They were shivering from the cold and fear. She immediately opened the door and slowly started making her way towards them. It was a bit far away as she placed it in the middle of the field. She made sure not to slip and fall. Steve was going with her. They were trying to be as quick as possible when suddenly, a bolt of lightning hit the rod. The pigs were hugging the rod, and they were hit as well. They transformed into these hideous zombie-like creatures. Their front limbs grew into arms, and they were standing on two feet. Half of their body turned into a skeleton, and they had green infections like the zombies. This was what Alex was afraid would happen. She was so shocked that she started crying. She couldn't take a look at them anymore. She started blaming herself. "What have I done?"

"If I hadn't placed it there, they wouldn't have come near it and got hit by the lightning. What will I do now? Oh no..." The Pigmen soon fled from there as they were probably very confused about what had happened. Alex was devastated and couldn't think properly. Steve kept telling her that it would be fine. "We will figure something out. Worrying won't get you anywhere." But it didn't comfort Alex one bit. "I will find a way to fix them," Steve promised her.

Steve's first idea was to go back to the village. The librarian knew about a lot of things, so she should also know about the pigmen. He also thought about the cleric. He was into weird stuff, so he should know about it as well. But the problem was the rain. It wouldn't take them too long to go to the village, but they couldn't start their journey at that moment. So, they had to wait for the rain to stop. He kept trying to comfort Alex but didn't succeed. It was going to be a long day.

After what felt like a decade, the rain was finally stopping. Meanwhile, Alex made a few cookies to calm herself a bit and it kind of worked. She got herself together. She understood that it wasn't the time to sit around and cry. She had made a mistake, and she had to fix it.

Steve was quite surprised to see her preparing like that. She borrowed Steve's brand new full set of iron armor. She asked him to make her a bow and a new sword. He did as she said, and she was ready. Steve had to make his preparations and went to his house to do so. Alex made an extremely responsible decision of not taking any cakes on her. Instead, she made bread, three stacks of bread. She was fully prepared to do whatever it took to save her pigs.

Steve wore his armor and took his sword. He also took his book and decided that he would ask the toolsmith to put the enchant on his sword. He took his bow, arrows, and food. He took two extra water buckets because it's better to take precautions. He had his diamond pickaxe and was completely geared out and ready to go.

They headed out towards the village as fast as they could. The sky was getting dark again. It was going to be a big problem if it started to rain again. They quickened their pace as much as they could. Just as they were getting out of the oak forest, it started to rain again. This time it wasn't as heavy as before. They took the risk and kept going. They had to use the boat to get there faster, but the problem was they would be exposed. So, they had to hope that there wouldn't be a thunderstorm again.

Things were going smoothly, and they reached the end of the river quite quickly. The rain was gradually stopping, but the sun was going down. The night wasn't a big problem for them as they got a bit used to it. After what happened in the cave, they were ready for anything.

They kept going through the jungle. It was night, so it was a bit difficult, but they managed. They were sprinting through everything. The only slight concern Steve had was about food. He didn't know that Alex had brought bread this time. He was wondering if she had run out of food. He asked her, but she said she was fine. So, he believed her and kept going.

Soon they were out of the jungle. It was almost dawn. The sun was peeking over the horizon. They were near the mountain range. And that meant that they were nearing the village. They headed straight between the gap of two of the mountains. It was a narrow path but made it a lot easier for them. It meant that they didn't have to climb the whole thing. They quickly passed the mountains and saw the village. They soon made their way towards it.

Alex had another concern on her way to the village. The pigmen fled very quickly. They had to find them again. But then she thought that it would be pointless to search for them without knowing how to cure them. She reassured herself that she would do everything to cure them. After all, she was the reason they became like that.

It was a bit after dawn. The villagers had already woken up. The weaponsmith was out near the edge of the village, feeding the golems. He noticed Steve and was pleasantly surprised. He saw that they were running really fast. He approached Steve and asked, "Hey, are ye okay? What happened? You look really pale." Steve replied, "Alex's pigs turned into this weird zombie-like thingy. We are trying to figure out how to cure them. Do you know anything about it?"

"Go visit the cleric." The weaponsmith immediately suggested. "He is the oldest of all the villagers and knows a lot about things." He would travel all the time, and rumors had it that he had also visited another dimension! But the cleric was going to go out again that day. So, the weaponsmith told them to quickly go there or else they might miss him.

Steve told Alex, "Go to the stone tower and find the cleric before he leaves. If we don't catch him, we might be in trouble." He would talk to the librarian and try to find out more about the pigmen. Alex immediately headed towards the Stone tower as Steve proceeded to go to the librarian's place.

He quickly went to her house and knocked on the door. The librarian opened it and greeted him. "I thought you went back to your base," she told him. "We did, but we ran into some trouble," he replied. Steve then proceeded to explain what happened and how lightning hit some of Alex's beloved pigs. He further explained how the pigs then turned into this zombie pigman. The librarian listened carefully.

She then replied, "I don't know why it happens, but it happened to one of the farmer's pigs as well." The pigman didn't seem hostile. He would just hang around, but one day he was gone. "Do you know the cure?" Steve asked. "Unfortunately, I don't. It might not be possible. But visit the cleric. He might know something," she suggested.

Steve thanked the librarian and wanted to head towards the cleric. But he decided to make another stop. He wanted to use his enchanted book to further enchant his iron sword. The toolsmith's place was near the librarian's house. So, he quickly went there.

The toolsmith was doing something on the anvil. Steve approached and greeted him. He explained, "I am in a bit of a hurry. Can you enchant his iron sword?" The toolsmith agreed and took his sword and the book. He then proceeded to put them on his anvil and started doing something. "It would still take a bit of time," he told Steve. So, he had to wait.

Chapter 19: Transdimensional Journey

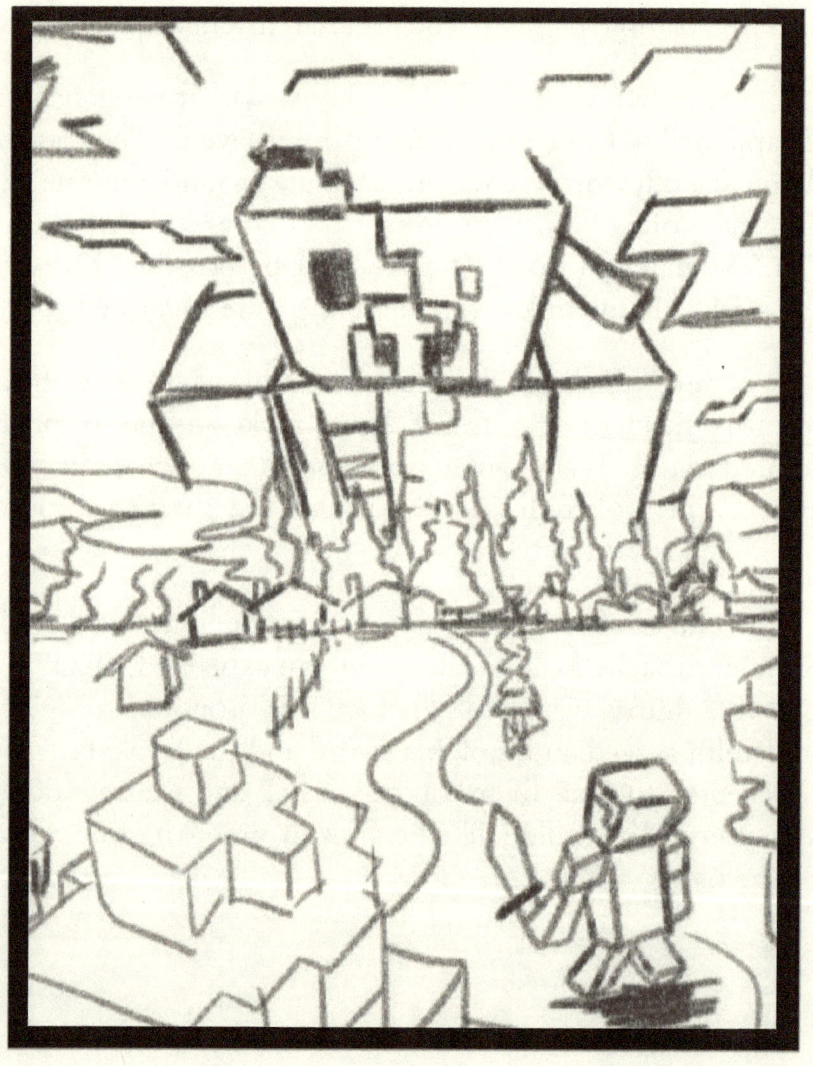

Alex was sprinting as fast as she could. She couldn't miss the cleric. If she did, she would lose her only way of finding the cure of the zombie pigman. She soon saw the stone tower and saw that the cleric was leaving. She screamed, calling the cleric. "Hey, wait, WAIIIT!" The cleric stopped and saw that Alex was rushing towards him. He got concerned and asked her, "What happened? Why are you back so soon? Is everything alright?" "No, I am in some trouble," Alex replied. She then told the cleric about how her pigs turned into zombie pigmen. After hearing the description of the pigmen, the cleric said that he had seen them in only one place. "The pigmen aren't the mobs of the overworld. I only ever saw them in the nether."

The nether was a hellscape of a dimension. The cleric was the only one to ever go there. He had found a portal made by the people of the forgotten ages. He used to roam a bit in the nether and come back. He never got the courage to explore it too deeply. One day, something strange happened. The portal frame broke. It spooked him out enough that he didn't fix it and never had gone there since.

Alex was intimidated by the thought of going into another dimension. She had to discuss it with Steve. Just as she was thinking about him, Steve ran up to her. She asked her, "Did you find anything?" She told him about the other dimension and what the cleric told her. The cleric proceeded to tell him more about this other dimension. "There are lots and lots of zombie pigmen there. If you want to go there, you might find a clue on how to cure them."

The cleric knew where the portal was and how to fix it. He told them that he could activate the portal again. But in return, they had to do something. "Bring me anything unusual you find in the Nether. I would love to research them." They agreed, and the cleric started leading the way. The portal was in the ocean. It was a bit further up north of the village. The cleric was navigating the way. He had a map and had marked the location.

While they were walking, Steve got a bit nervous. Was it a good decision to agree to go into a totally different dimension? They decided it in a hurry. Steve started to doubt the choice. But then again, he couldn't just sit around doing nothing. He had to find a way to help Alex because she was always by his side. And now he can't just leave her alone. He knew even if there was a tiny chance of curing the pigs, Alex would do everything to find it, even if it meant going to another dimension. Thinking too much would get him nowhere. If Alex wanted to go to the nether and find a cure for her pigs, he would do the same. He made that decision, and there was no going back.

The cleric was faster than he looked. He was navigating the map as if he knew it like the back of his hand. He was quick to make corrections and was amazing at finding weird pathways. He held a compass in one hand and the map in the other. Steve would ask him to teach him how he did it. Of course, he wouldn't get the chance now, but he kept it on his bucket list.

They finally approached the ocean. "Get on your boats. It will be faster than swimming. The portal is a bit further into the ocean." Steve already had one, and so did the cleric. They got onto their boats and followed the cleric. He went straight for a bit, and they could see the portal frame. A huge dark purple frame and at its bottom were blocks Steve had never seen before. It looked like the other dimension started to spread into theirs.

They reached the portal, and the frame was made up of obsidian. Steve expected it to be some otherworldly unnatural block, but nope, it was your plain old obsidian. He also noticed that some of the obsidian looked a bit different, and the frame itself was incomplete. A few blocks were missing. The cleric placed the missing obsidian and used a flint and steel to light it up.

Steve and Alex both took a deep breath. They were actually going to do it. They were going to the nether. The cleric told them to double-check their gears. Steve made sure his sword was sharp, which it was because the toolsmith enhanced it. Alex checked her trusty bow. The strings were tight, and her shield was spotless. "You ready, Alex?" Steve asked. "I am ready," she replied without skipping a beat.

The cleric gave them some final warnings. "If you feel that it is getting too dangerous, you have to head back into the portal immediately." He also told them to make a trail so that they don't forget where the portal was. This was it. Alex was determined to find out what was up with the pigmen. The cleric gave them some final words of encouragement.

"It might seem more dangerous than it actually is. But never let your guard down. Trust in your instincts and judge situations properly. And finally, good luck and be careful."

"Thank you, Carl, for helping us," Steve thanked him one last time. "Let's go, Alex." They got their thoughts together. They didn't know what was inside the portal. They had no idea what dangers were waiting for them. They knew nothing except the words from the mouth of the cleric. Even though they knew the odds stacked against them, they stepped forward into the portal. They braced themselves for the unknown territory of the Nether.

HELP A FELLOW READER

Take part in helping your fellow readers by sharing how you have liked the book so far. Your reviews help other readers make a sound and informed decision before placing an order. Did you love the book? Are you recommending it to a friend? Leave your reviews and comments on Amazon for everyone's notice. Thank you, and we look forward to receiving them.

BOOK RECOMMENDATION

The Journals of Steve

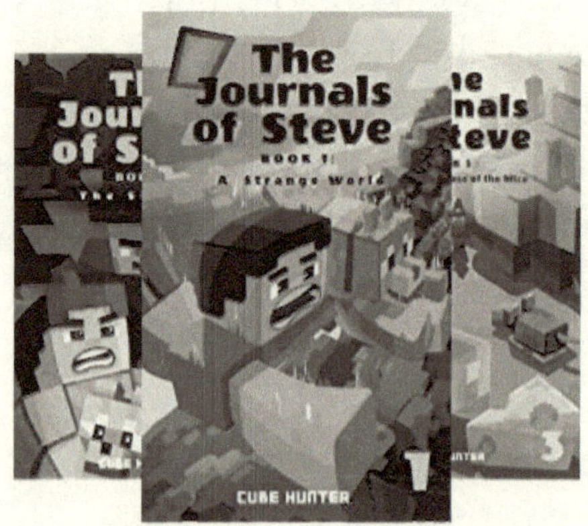

Life Of A Piglin: The Day Steve Came To Visit

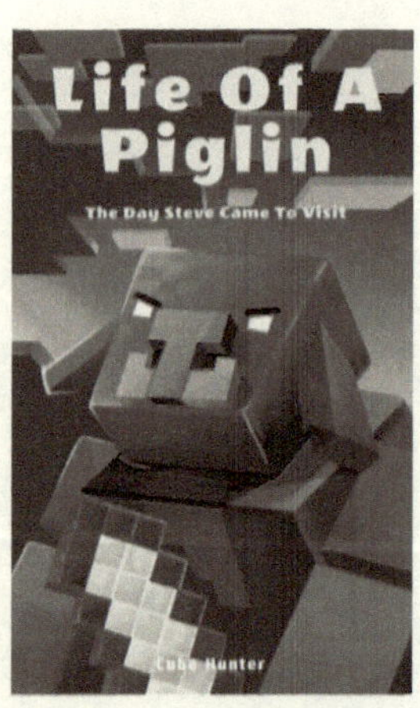

www.ingramcontent.com/pod-product-compliance
Lightning Source LLC
Chambersburg PA
CBHW022000150726
47990CB00002B/537